Angels Behind Bars

HOMERO RODRIGUEZ

To my beloved brothers and sisters in prison,
to my family and friends, thanks for your inspiration;
thank you, Lord, for guiding me;
Father Jablonski, thank you for your unconditional support.

CHAPTER ONE

I gasp for fresh air but this cell is so small and filthy that it's hard to breathe. I feel lonely and exhausted; fed up with constantly being told what to do; drained of being humiliated by the whole system. I hate not being able to receive proper medical treatment. I'm tired of having to wait for everything. I long to be with my family and everyone I love.

The cell seems to shrink as the minutes pass. Drops of cold sweat begin to run down my forehead. A heavy, dark shadow falls over me. Death enters my cell as I weep bitterly and begin to tie a rope around my neck. I gaze up, trembling.

"Please, God! Show me your face!" I demand furiously with a cracking voice. "I'm tired of all this. Please come down and save me from this misery!"

The heaviness of my tears burns my gaunt face and a horrible lump in my throat asphyxiates me.

"Take this pain! Take this loneliness away!" I shout at God between soul-shredding sobs.

There is neither response nor silence because the pounding of my heart echoes and permeates into the walls with my heavy breathing. I look up once again but this time I ask God for forgiveness.

"I'm sorry, but I can't live like this." I wipe off my tears with both hands and then throw myself to the ground from the upper bunk. My body hangs suspended in the air, twitching painfully, as if refusing to leave this world. Suddenly, everything begins to turn dark, then white, and then a shimmering light seems to strike my entire being with a mighty force. My body loses its strength.

Then after a moment of torture and suffering, the rope rips and my body crashes to the concrete. I instantly pant for air and cry again miserably, cursing God as I lay in a fetal position.

I remain on the cold floor for hours until I finally manage to stand up and let myself collapse on the lower bunk, lost in anguish. My restless heart longs for something, but I don't know exactly what it is. It's always like this. I need someone to hold me; I need a loving embrace, a compassionate friend; a mother; someone to tell me that I'm loved and forgiven. I feel helpless, forgotten, restless, and empty because I'm missing out on so much of life. I'm scared. I don't want to spend the rest of my life in prison, neglected and ignored, left to die alone in the darkness and bitterness of a cell.

The place feels darker and colder. I want to take a nap but my body refuses. The guard walks from cell to cell with his tiny flashlight in one hand and a bunch of mail in the other. He shoots the light right at me through the small-square window on the metal door. I get up, still gasping, and watch carefully to see if he slides a letter under the door. He passes my cell. No mail again.

I sit on the floor facing my bunk, rubbing off the redness caused by the cord around my neck. I pull my hair backwards as if trying to uproot it from the scalp.

"I hate it in here!" I yell with all my strength, but even the echo of my swearing seems to make fun of my sorrow. I pick up my foam sandals and toss them angrily against the wall. I slump by the door and stare a hole through the floor; then I find myself fixing my eyes on the ceiling for a while, motionless, with my mind suddenly lost in memories. After a while I get up to go to bed, pull the blankets up under my chin and at some point I fall asleep.

About an hour later, the thunderous voice of the guard penetrates my eardrums with the usual four o'clock count time. I get up and stand by the bunk as the officer shines a light through the window. When the count clears, the cell doors are immediately unlatched. I push the gray, iron door open and glance around the common area.

Everything is the same. The metal benches and tables are in the same place, rooted like trees. The imposing white walls still meet each other in the corners of the unit, with the same ominous steel handrails around the tiers. The television plays the same shows. The inmates, whose white outfits fuse with the walls, still walk around like sheep without a shepherd. And the dark cloud of indifference in the guards overshadows the block again. Every time I come out of my cell, the day room is suddenly filled with feelings of sadness, loneliness, anger, hatred, distrust, and vengeance. There is always an invisible, huge wave of tension that seems to crush us all.

I want to sit down but all the tables are taken at once. I wander around for a while with a sour taste in my mouth, feeling as if the weight of a mountain is pressing down on me. Everyone is busy with their own business. Some of the guys play cards, chess, or dominoes, while others just kill time watching TV. My cell unit is small, crowded, and always filled with gossip, rumors and scandals. It's a small world and all of us are very aware of our surroundings, paying attention to the tiniest and seemingly insignificant details around us.

I walk towards the TV area with my head hanging but I freeze when I see a naked middle-aged man get out of his cell in desperation, tearing off the pages of the Bible, one by one in extreme anxiety. A blinding wrath makes him jump on the surface of a metal table and scream with a commanding voice, "God is dead! And we are his murderers! Yes, you and I have killed Him. Look around you, there is nothing left of God in any of us." He squeezes his left fist until his knuckles turn white and clenches his teeth as he flings the Bible to the floor. Then he turns his head around, now with a tormented expression on his face, and his sight suddenly freezes on mine, leaving me paralyzed.

Everyone in the block is shocked by the strange scene. Some laugh at him and mock his last words; others just glance and keep on doing their own thing, but the eyes of the more religious men grow bigger in disbelief. Officer Serrano walks towards the madman to take control.

"Get off the table!" the huge, bald officer yells as he pulls his taser gun and points it at him.

"But don't you understand?" the madman insists, unable to control his tremulous hands while tears border his eyelids, "God's own creations have turned against Him. He's now dead; we've killed Him."

"Shut up and get back to your cell!" The guard snaps back, annoyed by his words which raise his adrenaline and anger to the point that his eyes look like they're going to pop out of their sockets. The inmate remains immobile, standing on the table like a statue, defying the authority in front of him with a sudden silence and a frightening grimace. Officer Serrano explodes gripping his ankle and pulling him down with the strength of someone whose anger is utterly out of control. He gives him a slap that makes him fall to the ground like a rag doll; he kicks his back once, twice, and then spits on him, yelling all kinds of things. After shuddering painfully for a few seconds, with his eyes closed, the prisoner manages to stand up between exaggerated moans and obeys the guard's order like a miserable walking zombie.

After witnessing with contempt the deplorable scene, everyone goes back again to their own business. I'm not really shocked by Serrano's usual abusive behavior as I am by the madman's accusation, which penetrates my heart like a cold dagger. I shake my head and give officer Serrano a look that could kill. Then as I stroll to the restroom, several men fiercely block my way.

"Hey, wuz up, Mikey" snarls T.J., a guy from Tijuana who used to sell me drugs, "got my thing yet?" He stares at me with a challenging look as he slightly strikes his left fist against his right hand. Two of his men stand behind him with a searing glare. My feet want to flee back to the cell but they know it will only make things worse, so I dare to confront his intimidating stance.

"You know I ain't got that much money right now," I utter, lifting my chin as a sign of defiance, "I told you I'd pay back next month."

He sneers at me, cracking his neck as if getting ready to punch me in the face but is pulled slightly away by one of his bodyguards who signals him to be careful because the officer is watching.

"I'm comin' back at you." He threatens, pointing his finger at me as he leaves.

I curse at him in my head and sigh, running my fingers through my hair.

"Hey, Michael, you wanna join our Bible study?" shouts Eddie, a black, heavy young dude, waving his hand, sitting with a small crowd. He is about my age, probably a bit younger, maybe in his late twenties. I'm a bit surprised when he calls me by name.

"Yeah, come on over, bro," encourages another guy as he squirms in the bench. I hesitate a little while staring blankly at Eddie for a few seconds.

"I'm gonna go take a piss, I'll be right back," I respond, faking I'm interested. The truth is I don't feel like listening to what I believe is pure hypocrisy. I finish doing my thing but have no intention to join their table. I go around them instead and sit with another throng to watch TV. The religious guys look at me but no one insists me to be part of their gathering.

My mind begins to wander in unknown territory, very far from the world of the living, while my eyes become hypnotized by whatever is on the TV. Then Serrano breaks my mental delusions with his vociferous order to get ready for dinner. We all get in line and, like a large herd of cattle, walk to the chow hall for the typical tasteless meal.

After dinner, I go back to my cell and remain sitting on the edge of my bunk, immobile, in silence, staring off into space. My face is bent down and my hands clasped together. Grief begins to envelop me again. I glance around. I feel I'm lacking air. Suicidal thoughts come back to haunt me. I close my eyes and hide my face while pacing back and forth clumsily. Then I curl up in a corner and begin to sob with remorse. The tears of guilt, which I believe are the most painful, mercilessly burn my cheeks. I put both hands on my head and pull my hair violently without feeling any pain.

"Our Father who art in heaven," I pray, trembling, "hallowed be thy name…" I can't even speak but I finish the prayer in my thoughts. I try to appease the emotional confusion by splashing some water on my face, but it's useless, the darkness of the cell seems to take over me once again. A deep sadness invades my soul as I slouch on the lower bunk. For hours I toss and turn trying desperately to get some sleep. I don't know why but I force myself to say a few other prayers, and at some point I do fall asleep.

Morning comes. I don't feel like waking up for breakfast at five in the morning, so after eight I get up, grab my towel, and walk out of the cave with a million thoughts swirling around in my head. I stand in front of the toilet to take a piss when I suddenly hear a voice coming from the shower stalls, "Hey, bro, how ya doin'?" It's Eddie nagging again, scrubbing his head as he hums a religious song with an exaggerated joy.

"God bless you, brother!" he insists when he gets no response from me.

"I'm cool, man, thanks," I answer, concealing annoyance.

"You gonna join us this time for Bible study?"

"Bible study? Dude, do I look like I'm interested in wasting my time with you, hypocrite fools?" I don't say that, I simply picture myself saying it.

"You there?"

"I'll think about it, man," I reply, forcing myself to sound respectful. Then he finally zips his mouth and steps out of the shower. We exchange a fake smile as I begin to undress and carefully go in the shower, trying to avoid a small area of the concrete floor covered with dirt and fungus.

The freezing water usually bristles my skin, but all I feel right now is a thin stream threading down my body like tears. The beating of my heart seems to stop as I listen, immobile, to the gurgling of the water for a long time. When I finish, I get dressed and stroll back to my cell, but on my way there, I hear the main door of the unit slide open. I stop and slightly tilt my body to see who it is. Everyone does the same.

It is a new inmate carrying with great difficulty a bedroll under his arm and a dirty sack hanging over his shoulder. He is escorted by a guard who immediately removes the steel cuffs and the chain binding his ankles. As if he had just delivered a package, the escorting officer shakes Serrano's hand and provides him information about the new inmate; then he disappears. The newcomer pulls out his ID card and hands it over to Serrano who in turn supplies him with a few hygiene items and reluctantly offers some instructions. The inmate follows his directions and heads towards cell 12A on the lower level, slightly smiling, with his head held high. A multitude of eyes are watching him and countless prying ears adjust their frequency towards him. He inspects the place moving his head right to left as if trying to find someone he knows. He holds his belongings clutched to his chest and doesn't seem scared or indifferent like other inmates when they first arrive. I scan him carefully from top to bottom without realizing that cell 12A is my own cell. My jaw drops and my eyes pop out in disbelief.

"What the…" I growl, squeezing my towel with both hands. I immediately go after him with the absurd intention to stop him from invading my space.

"Excuse me" I shout with a threatening voice. The man stops in his tracks and turns around. His *cholo*[1] appearance and the look on his face tell me he isn't intimidated by anything, though he doesn't seem either like other inmates who are always on edge, ready to kick someone's ass.

"Yeah, what's up, bro?" the inmate utters softly. He's definitely Hispanic, probably in his mid-thirties, and maybe six feet tall. His well-built body, shaved head, and quite a few tattoos sticking out of his short sleeves could easily scare the crap out of anybody. I really don't know what else to say.

"You gonna be in 12A, too?" I finally ask, toughening my voice a little.

"Yeah," he answers again in a gentle tone, turns around and walks into the room while I remain outside grumbling, thinking how this man has just screwed up my little privacy.

"So who's the new guy," I hear a husky voice behind me. It's this black man, Big Bear.

"I don't know, man." I respond with a gesture of irritation as I enter my cave. I put my towel down on the lower bunk as if to mark my territory.

"You get the top bunk," I utter firmly.

"Yeah, no problem," he responds, taking the stuff out of his sack and placing it into the upper locker. He unrolls his thin piece of mattress and gingerly lays it out on the top, solid base. I leave the cell to chill with my homeboys out in the day

---

[1] gangster

room for a while, but the tension that always lingers around the unit makes me go back inside. I grab my radio and sit down for some time, speechless.

When lunch time is announced, I gather with my homeboys in the common area, then we all head to the crowded chow hall for the meal. From the corner of my eyes I notice my cellie walking towards our table. The homeboys stare at him with a welcoming look. One of them motions him to sit down.

"Yo, what up. What's your name?" asks my friend Flaco, a Mexican youngster, with a somewhat friendly tone as he examines his meal with suspicion.

"Emmanuel," the new inmate responds, dropping his body on the metal bench, "but my homeboys call me Manu."

We all shake hands with him and continue eating, repugnantly, our tasteless bologna sandwich. Emmanuel remains quiet throughout the whole meal, listening to our conversation, which is loaded with pure macho crap. As my homeboys and I boast about how tough we are, our guest smiles once in a while, apparently enjoying his insipid sandwich. He must be really hungry; I had never seen anybody devour a bologna sandwich with such delight before.

"You got some badass tattoos there, fool," Flaco articulates, pointing at my cellie's forearms covered with gothic letters and other religious images that are difficult to distinguish at first sight.

"Thanks, bro," Emmanuel answers with his mouth still stuffed.
"Where'd you get 'em?"

And here we go again, another superficial conversation. I'm tired of listening to the same old crap. Why can't we talk about other things, things that don't involve people's appearance? Why can't we look into each other's interior and take the time to listen to the wailing of our hearts? I hate humanity for this.

I spend the rest of the afternoon doing absolutely nothing, except thinking about my well-deserved punishment for the stupid decisions I've made and the pain I inflicted on others. If the goal of incarceration is to kill the soul, they're doing a remarkable job.

The day comes to an end with our dinner. It is always like this. The irony of ironies is that even though time seems to pass, there is no evolution within these walls. Our little world is full of the same routines, yet at the same time full of uncertainty.

I feel bored and lazy. I yawn once in a while, exaggerating a little. My cellie reads a book and doesn't pay attention to my laziness. We haven't really exchanged a formal conversation since he joined the unit this morning. I want to break the silence but I hold back. Instead, I remove my nasty white khakis, pull my hair backwards and go to bed.

"Hey, bro, good night," Emmanuel exclaims as I begin to doze off. I'm rather surprised by his gesture, but I remain mute.

CHAPTER TWO

Today is Wednesday, but the days don't matter here; they're always the same for those of us who don't get any visits or any letters. I still feel like trash, though; like a miserable human being trapped in a world full of lies and pains. It hurts having to pretend to be someone I'm not. I'm tired of playing the tough guy in front of everyone when in the depths of my heart I ache for a loving embrace.

"Hey, *ese*,[2]" yells Flaco from the other end of the unit, sitting his ass on a steel bench. The other homeboys, Elmo, Smiley, and Vaquero, sit beside him quietly but somewhat anxious. I walk towards them without realizing the fate that awaits me.

"Better watch out, *loco*," Flaco immediately explains. "I ran into that fool over there," he points discreetly with his eyes at Necio, the leader of one of the gangs in this unit, "he said you better watch your back, fool."

I sit down, pulling my hair backwards with both hands. I know I'm in deep trouble and aware of what's about to happen.

"What's goin' on, homie?" Flaco inquires, "I thought you two were homeboys."

---

[2] dude, 'fool'

"Look, ya'll," I utter, avoiding his question, without really knowing what to say. "I know we been hanging out for a while now, and I appreciate all you done for me. But I think it's best if I stay out of your way." They look puzzled but I continue, "Seriously, I don't wanna get you in trouble and delay your release cuz of me. Ya'll have families out there to take care of. I ain't got nobody, so I ain't got nothing to lose. Ya'll keep it up."

I get up to go to the restroom area but Flaco follows me.

"Hey, man," he calls out, "whatcha talkin' bout? What was that all about?"

"Necio's got some issues with me."

"I know, fool, but what exactly is goin' on with you two?"

"It's a long story, bro, just try to be safe."

"Look, homie, I don't know what the hell is happenin', but if you need anythin' you know I'm down for ya."

"Thanks, man, I know that." I whisper. Then we shake hands and he joins the rest at the table.

The trustees show up in the unit with some brown paper bags for lunch. My cellie heads to Flaco's table but stops in his tracks when he perceives my intention to cage myself and have lunch in the swamp of the cell. He greets Flaco and the others with a nod and then turns around to follow my footsteps.

"I thought you'd be sitting with Flaco and the others," he states entering the cell.

"No, not this time," I respond, irritated.

"I thought you guys…"

"Look, *ese*, I'm not having a good day, aright?"

Manu apologizes and places his meal on his bunk. He could have smashed the brown bag right on my face for the way I spoke to him but he didn't. There's definitely something different about this man. He looks intently at the wall while slowly biting on his sandwich, as if he were counting how many chews it takes to disintegrate.

I finish the crappy, tasteless sole-looking ham sandwich and, without saying anything, I leave the cell to approach the TV area that has already been surrounded by a lively, yet impatient throng that loudly cheers for their football team. I sit on the floor for about half an hour. The inmates' uproar irritates officer Martinez who immediately orders the men to shut up and keep some order.

"God bless you, brother!" Eddie exclaims as he passes by in a hurry, waving goodbye. My cellie walks behind him with a bunch of books under his arm. I think they're going to church. Again. I raise my eyebrows to acknowledge his greeting, then I get up to lock myself in the cave.

I sit on the floor and remain motionless for several minutes. I grab a small pencil and toy with it, tracing some silly squiggles on a piece of paper. I gaze up and stare at my cellie's property, which is neatly ordered in his locker. Then I'm suddenly seized by some strange curiosity. My feet straighten up and jump to the door to make sure no one is coming. I sift through Emmanuel's belongings very carefully but all he has is books, some snacks, and more books.

"What the…," I groan, like a child who's been denied a promised candy. As I put everything back in order, I notice a yellowed, fraying envelope stashed behind a bunch of religious magazines. I grab it immediately and empty out its content in a hurry. I count seven letters, twelve photos and three folded fragments of newspaper. I glance at each photo but it's hard to tell what's on them; the images are warped and blurry. I flip them over to see if they have an inscription but they don't. I walk towards the window again. The deafening racket for the football game continues. Before I stuff everything back in the envelope, I gingerly unfold the fractions of newspaper and glimpse at them but nothing remarkable captures my interest. Then I open the letters, one by one, until the retina in my eyes reacts to a beautiful handwriting. I contemplate the manuscript for seconds, and as I read the title, the intercom interrupts my concentration with the code that desperately demands the presence of the squad in my unit.

"What the heck is going on?" I murmur, peeking through the tiny glass. It's hard to see what's going on, all I hear is people cursing at each other. It's probably another fight over a stupid football game.

I lean on the door and unfold the piece of paper. The rancid smell of the toilet reaches my nostrils but I don't pay much attention to it; the content is not long:

THE TEN PRISON COMMANDMENTS

-THOU SHALL PRAY FOR YOUR FELLOW INMATES, ALL OF THEM.
-THOU SHALL NOT JUDGE ANYONE.
-BE AWARE OF THE POWER OF YOUR WORD.
-BE PATIENT WITH GOD AND WITH YOURSELF.
-THE PAST CANNOT BE CHANGED; FOCUS ON THE HERE AND NOW.
-STOP FEELING SORRY FOR YOURSELF.
-NEVER JOIN A GANG.
-STOP COMPLAINING AND BLAMING OTHERS FOR EVERYTHING THAT GOES WRONG IN YOUR LIFE.
-THOU SHALL NOT WASTE YOUR TIME.
-COUNT YOUR BLESSINGS BEFORE YOU GO TO BED.

"What a load of crap," I protest, shaking my head. I hold the letter a few seconds, then turn it over a couple of times to see if it has a sender's name, but it doesn't. Then I put the paper down as I try to collect my thoughts. I feel tired and frustrated, pacing around in an effort to wipe out a disturbing drizzle of memories that seems to crush my mind. I put everything back in the envelope, then I toss myself on the bunk, hearing with extreme irritation the heavy steps of the squad running around the unit like enraged beasts, trying to disentangle the conflict between the cheering crowds.

After a little while, the intercom announces that the quarrel has been finally resolved by the troop, which consequently punishes the whole block by locking everyone down.

"Oh, God, not again." I grunt drowsily.

Sometime later, Manu comes back from Church, right before the four o'clock count begins, and immediately asks about the fight.

"What fight?" I reply sluggishly.

"Code two is for fights, and it happened in our unit just a…"

"Oh yeah, the code," I interrupt, still half asleep.

He puts his book in his locker and grabs another one. Then he climbs up to his bunk and begins to read while I try to fall back asleep. A growling noise coming from my stomach makes me get up and sit on the cold, steel toilet. "Damn sandwich," I whisper, frowning. When I finish, I pull off my shirt and hurl myself to the ground for some exercise, hoping to diminish the stress. I do push-ups and sit-ups repeatedly until I run out of breath; then I crumple on my bunk to rest a while.

"Hey, homie, you want a snack?" asks my reticent cellie, hopping down from his bunk, "I got some peanut butter cookies and some Cheetos."

"Really?" I respond incredulously, yet with a slight tone of gratitude. I dry the sweat off my body with a torn, white towel while he hands me a small bag of cookies, which I devour in less than a minute. I lick my fingers and glance at the Cheetos my cellie is about to open.

"You want some Cheetos, too, bro?" he asks, now looking at me with a grin. "Here, man." He tosses me his bag and takes another one for him.

"Thanks, bro. I really appreciate it," I express timidly,

with a ripple of regret for my apathetic attitude towards him.

"No problem."

Emmanuel crawls back up to his bunk. The crunching of both his and my Cheetos is like background music in the ever frightening silence of the cell. I intend to make some conversation but I don't want to be perceived as needing to talk to someone or that I feel lonely. But after several minutes of staring blankly at the bottom of my cellie's bunk, munching, and licking my fingers, I push myself to defy the evil atmosphere disguised as quietness with a question, "So where you from, bro?"

I hear my cellie slide his back toward the wall, in a more comfortable position, as if getting ready for a long conversation.

"I'm from San Antonio, Texas," he answers. "Well, I was born there, but I've been moving around for quite a while. Part of my family still lives there, though."

He pauses as if expecting me to react to his words but I don't. "How 'bout you?" he adds.

I get up, sit on the edge of my bunk, and rub my hands through my hair. "I was born in Dallas, but my parents come from Mexico. I been chillin' all over Texas, too. You know, doin' business here and there, just tryin' to make a livin'."

My cellie listens carefully, staring at the damp-patched wrinkled wall.

"Did you ever kick it in San Anton?" he inquires when the cell is conquered again by the ominous silence.

"Yeah, I was there for a few years."

"I see," he sighs, sensing a sudden lack of interest from my part in our dialogue.

"Listen, bro," he states, "I don't know what got you here, but I want you to know you got a brother right here. You can call me Manu."

"What?" I murmur to myself, finding it difficult to believe in such a premature declaration. Everybody around here has a different mask for every situation and for every person. I know full well that trusting someone in here is like giving a gun to your enemy. This place is a jungle in which only the aggressive and strongest survives. I refuse to be the prey, the weak.

I raise my eyes to look at my cellie. His tough, yet mysterious countenance tells me he's not like everyone else. There is something genuinely peaceful about this guy.

"Thanks, man," I force myself to respond with a croaky voice. We spend the rest of the afternoon in our cells, without dinner. The lockdown goes on till the following day.

"I'm glad you don't snore, bro," Manu jokes with a silly grin plastered across his face when he realizes I'm awake. He throws his baggy, white shirt on the floor and yawns, exaggerating a bit.

"You know," I utter, "actually, I should also thank you for that cuz I don't think you snore either."

He chuckles.

"That means good sleep all the time," he adds, flashing his perfect teeth; then he jumps down and sits on the steel toilet. He has a beautiful detailed image of the crucifixion tattooed on his back.

"Hey, that's a nice tat!" I exclaim.

"Thanks."

"I'm gonna take a shower, man," I announce, gripping my towel.

There it is, again; the dayroom flooded with the same of everything. The sun is rarely seen from inside the block, but on this occasion its rays seem to disintegrate the thick, stained little windows. Mr. Johnson, nicknamed Grandpa, is contemplating the blurry view of the sun, allowing its beams to sting his cheeks. Although he's the oldest in the unit, his nickname doesn't just refer to his old age, it's also about his years in prison; some say he's been here forever. The wrinkles on his face, his wisdom, and his peaceful behavior have gained him much respect in the prison.

"Hey, *mijo*,[3]" Grandpa cries out when he observes I'm gazing at him. "Come over here. Smell this," he points with excitement at a very small crack on the wall through which a slight current of wind blows in. "It's the scent of Christmas," he remarks. I smile and slowly pass my nose by the fissure, smelling nothing but pure air.

"Hey, Mexican!" someone shouts angrily behind me. "Whatcha been up to, *ese*? When ya gonna do the job, huh?" he asks, infuriated, with bloodshot eyes. Grandpa disappears with a feeling of helplessness when Necio shoves me up with both hands. His name is Ignacio, but everyone calls him Necio, and the only word that describes this *vato loco*[4] very well is tough. Necio is the toughest of the tough in the unit, hard as rock; he seems to have no fragile spots. Other men can cry and snivel, but not Necio. He spills waves of fear as he swaggers around the block with his crew, flaunting his toughness like a peacock shows off its flowing plumes. Necio is one of those who frown at any sign of weakness, taking advantage of the ones that show their emotions.

"I asked you something, *ese*!" he howls once again. He threatens me, like my father used to, pointing his index finger on my face as some of his followers stand behind him staring at me with contempt. I glance at officer Serrano in the glass box, hoping he will do something but he's, as usual, busy on the phone. The rest of the prisoners ignore with indifference the pitiful scene. Necio knows I can be as tough as him. He knows I'm not afraid of him. I lift my chin, grip the towel tight, and dip my eyes into the poison within me and throw an equally killing look at all of them.

---

[3] son
[4] crazy dude

"I'm gonna do that tomorrow, man, chill out..." I articulate after the exchange of a few glares. I don't know what to do. Necio breathes heavily, with a huge aura of superiority mixed with disgust. Several possible plans to kill him run through my head while some other prisoners begin to mutter among themselves, as if plotting to intervene in our confrontation.

"You know I don't play games. We'll be watching you, fool!"

Eddie and his Bible fellows notice my unfortunate confrontation from their table but don't say a word at the moment. After the shower, as I head back to my cell, Eddie comes up to me asking about the conflict and offering sincerely to help me, but I refuse to speak. I don't want him to pay the consequences as well.

"Whatever it is you going thru," he tells me, "talk to the officers, know what I'm saying? They can help you move out of here to another unit."

I stare at him for seconds, lost in anxiety. Eddie and I know very well I can't take that route; doing so will instantly mark me as a rat and a snitch forever, wherever I go. We both know that seeking protection from staff, especially from corrupted and indifferent ones, is not a reliable solution.

"Ok, I take that back," he states, as though he knows what's going through my head.

"But, man, how'd you get yourself entangled in such a mess?" He exclaims with a funny gesture.

Eddie's words echo in my feeble mind.

"Why don't you join our group, bro?" he adds, "they might as well leave you alone."

"Thanks for the advice," I utter, leaving him standing there. I know that if I don't do what they say the consequences will be irreparable.

I enter the cell with my head hanging. Manu sleeps again. The cell feels so cold my heart almost freezes. I sit down and take a deep breath but my lungs reject the nasty air that fills the cave. I cough covering my mouth with the towel. Paradoxically, I feel in hell.

"God, what am I gonna do?" I whisper, collapsing on the bunk, which produces an irritating screech that wakes my cellie up.

"Hey, man," Manu murmurs, lifting his head. "You alright?"

I feel like screaming and venting everything that has been confined in my heart for a long time, but a poisonous lump in my throat seems to asphyxiate me. This relentless frustration and anxiety have turned what's left of my heart into a rock. It's this wicked environment that's making me crazy.

"My soul craves for you, God," I utter in the silence and loneliness of my heart, "My soul thirsts for You. Please, help me. Why is my heart so disturbed?"

"Cellie?" Manu interrupts my thoughts.

As if motivated by an inner force, I dare to mumble, "Manu, it feels very lonely in here." I wait for his reaction with a crumbled spirit, but it seems my confession had no effect at all. Manu remains still on his bunk.

"Sometimes I feel the same way, Michael," he finally declares solemnly as I cover my face with a pillow. "Everything about this place increases our feeling of loneliness. But it doesn't always have to be that way." He comes down from his bunk and sits right beside me without permission.

"What do you mean?" I inquire.

"I've realized over the years that when we experience the pain of loneliness, we tend to respond either with arrogance and anger or with humility and love."

I frown at his words, unable to really understand what he meant.

Manu makes a slight pause, then continues with an exaggerated proper diction, "Many times, because of our loneliness, we take refuge in alcohol, drugs, sex, and many other vices that slowly kill the soul and, in many cases, lead us to suicide. We try so hard to fill the void of our hearts with things that only worsen our pain. This happens to those who react with arrogance and anger. These individuals feel superior to everyone else and hate everything that smells like God. Their arrogance makes them believe they don't need God or others. They're very selfish, closed minded, and refuse to hear any wisdom from others."

I rub my hands through my hair and sigh, knowing deep inside that I'm one of those individuals.

"I don't mean to disrespect, bro," I break in with a defensive argument, which is really more of a lie, "but no one has ever talked to me about God, so it's difficult to suddenly believe in someone who's been absent in my life, especially in the most painful moments."

"Sorry to hear that, homie," he tells me, his voice tinted with a slight disagreement about what I said.

"It's alright, I guess. So the thing you mentioned, about humility and love, what is it about?"

"We must begin by understanding that loneliness is nothing other than our thirst and hunger for God. All human beings were created to live in unity with God and with all of humanity; that's why as we go through life we are restless, dissatisfied and unhappy. There is a special tank in our hearts that only God's infinite love can fill.[5] Once we accept and embrace this basic truth we will be ready to respond with humility and love."

"Come on, Manu, " I intervene, "I understand what you're trying to tell me, but you're not expecting me to be

---

[5] Part of my own reflection on loneliness, as it appears in this novel, has been influenced by Ronald Rolheiser's extraordinary book, *The Restless Heart Finding Our Spiritual Home in Times of Loneliness* (New York: Doubleday, 2004).

humble around here, are you? If you show any sign of weakness, people will take advantage of you, and you know that."

Manu takes a few seconds to respond, knowing that what I said is true.

"I understand this environment is not the most suitable place to begin. But true humility is not about letting people take advantage of you, or going around begging others to beat you up. In this particular place, true humility is more about solidarity; it's having the conviction, the belief that all of us are in the same position, under the same predicament, and deserve to be treated with compassion and love. It's about respecting everyone else in what they do and in who they are, acknowledging their humanity and their suffering.

"All of us get tired of being humiliated and treated as mere inanimate objects checked into inventory. So as fellow prisoners, living under the same conditions and struggles, by embracing our loneliness with humility, rather than pride, we can learn to be more compassionate with one another because we speak the same language. We speak the language of loneliness and alienation. We can learn to treat each other with love because we speak and understand the language of suffering. Why do we always have to be defensive, aggressive, and with a tendency to look at our surroundings with suspicion, always expecting an enemy to suddenly appear and harm us? If we could only embrace our loneliness with humility and love, rather than running away from it or taking the route of the arrogant, we would be more capable of seeing our fellow prisoners as allies and friends who share in the same struggle and search for the same truth."

"Compassion and love?" I mock, shaking my head in disagreement, regarding his response as rather pious and sissy. "Come on, man, you can't be serious. These people don't care about those feelings."

"You sound much like many people in the free world,

Michael," my cellie states with an air of sadness, "Many people in society don't believe that prisoners can indeed experience a conversion of heart. Sadly, they see us as an everlasting threat. Even after release, our unforgiving society will remind you that you were once a rejected piece of trash, locked up in the middle of the wilderness. Understand this, Michael, if any prisoner ever sincerely wants to change his life, God is always willing to forgive him. And when we show compassion and love to our fellow prisoners, the same will be done to us."

Manu pauses to look deep into my eyes. I gaze back at him without realizing my mouth is a bit open, marveled at the way he speaks. I begin to pace back and forth. As I listen to my cellie's words, the walls around me, which for long seemed to boast of their thickness and strength, now give the impression of being thin and fragile.

"My brother," Manu continues, "loneliness is also an opportunity to appreciate even more our families and friends. A lot of times we go through life, especially out in the free world, taking things and persons for granted. We see life, friendship, health, and work as things that are owed to us. For this reason we fail to appreciate them and accept them with the love and respect they deserve. Instead of seeing them as precious gifts from God, we take them for granted. And sadly, most of us realize this behind bars.

"It's in our loneliness, Michael, that we learn that there's something greater than ourselves, that our own world and our own concerns are not all that there is, and that we're called to give ourselves for others. Sometimes, in our selfishness, we forget that we live in a world in which we're responsible for helping each other."

I sigh heavily, pulling my hair backwards, confused. Manu remains immobile on the edge of my bunk. Deep inside I know he is right about this whole thing, but it's so difficult to put into practice these concepts and truths. I pull my hair once again as I pace back and forth, feeling a strange desire to hear more.

"So you're saying God is the only one who can take this loneliness away?" I ask, twiddling with my baggy shirt.

"Many people get married hoping their loneliness will simply go away; others try to make a lot of friends to fill the void of their hearts, to decrease the pain of loneliness, but the truth is that if we don't allow God to fulfill that restless heart first, our relationships with others will always leave us with a sense of emptiness, a feeling of loneliness. Listen, Michael, no human being is ever able to destroy the loneliness and emptiness of another human heart because all human hearts are restless until they rest in God. Once our hearts are filled with God's infinite love, we can then begin to truly love and enjoy other human beings without the pain of loneliness."

I'm really moved by his words but I make sure it doesn't show. We gaze at each other intently, then I lean against the wall, breathing heavily, reflecting on his words. He is right. I always went through life trying to fill a spot in me that could not be filled, trying to quench a thirst that could not be quenched, and satisfy a hunger that could not be satisfied. But it wasn't my fault. I was a neglected child who grew up bitter and resentful, full of anger and hatred, unable to love because I could not erase the painful memories of my cruel childhood.

"All of us go through life longing to love and to be loved…" Manu continues as he stands up, but I'm so confused that I refuse to hear anything else.

"Look, man, thanks for the talk," I mumble, clearing my throat.
"We're not alone, Michael. Even when your family or your friends abandon you, know and be sure that God will never forsake you."

Manu puts his hand on my shoulder, and with this gesture I remain mute. There is no doubt that all those words came from his heart, but I struggle to understand his God of love and compassion. Why would God care about a man like me, after all the evil I've done?

I dive into bed and cover my ears with the radio headphones while Manu leaves the cell with his towel hanging over his shoulder. I stare at the brick wall facing my bunk, from corner to corner. I like looking at the dirt stains and the spots caused by water leaks; they form silly shapes of animals and distorted, funny faces. I really find it comforting.

CHAPTER THREE

"Hey, my friend," I hear Manu's words echo. "It's time for lunch."

I can't believe I slept again a few hours.

"Are you gonna go?"

"Yeah, I'll be up in a minute."

"Hey. I'm sorry if I said something that bothered you."

"Ain't nothing to be sorry about, homie," I offer, "everything you said is true. I guess I'm just not ready to accept it."

"Take all the time you need."

"I sure will."

I get up and put my clothes on. We do the usual line up and walk to the chow hall like wretched zombies. After waiting eternally in line for our meal, my cellie follows me and sits right in front of me. Flaco and my other homeboys pass by the table and quickly greet the two of us. Flaco returns in a hurry, and, with a ripple of excitement, whispers in my ear something that causes great relief.

"T.J. was shipped out to another unit; he beat the crap out of his cellie and was immediately transferred by the squad yesterday."

"What?"

"Yeah, man, he's not in our tank anymore. Remember code two yesterday when the football game was on?"

"Yeah."

"Well, it was for T.J. and his fight with his cellie. That fool won't be a problem anymore."

"Thanks for telling me, *ese*."

"No problem, *carnal*."

Manu looks at me a bit puzzled, intrigued by Flaco's mysterious whispering. I lower my head and apologize for the secretive chat.

"How long have you known those guys?" Manu asks, stuffing a piece of bread in his mouth.

"Not that long. They got here probably about seven months ago.

"Where they from?"

"Flaco is from Laredo, Mexico; he's the youngest of the group. The guy next to him, on his right, is from Honduras; we call him Elmo."

"The white guy is Gerardo, right?"

"Yeah, he's also from Mexico. The guys call him Vaquero. The short homeboy is Smiley; he's like the clown in the group, you always get a good laugh with him."

"They seem like good people."

"They are, man."

"So when did you join those other *vatos* in the gang?" he inquires, referring to Necio and his crew.

"That's another story, bro. And, to be honest, I don't wanna talk about it."

"It's alright, man. You don't have to."

A period of silence takes over between us. Manu seems like a good man. Although he has a tough, gangster appearance, his whole personality makes you want to trust in him. However, I'm still careful about what I share with him. It's this environment that kills the faith and hope in all human beings.

"Hey, bro," I break the silence, "do you really think God cares about people like us?"

"What do you mean 'people like us'?"

"Prisoners, murderers, rapists, thieves."

"That's a very easy question for some of us, yet quite difficult for others, and I could respond with a plain 'yes', but then you would not be satisfied with the answer. For us humans, it's very difficult to believe in a caring God, in a God of love and forgiveness. Because of our sins, our sufferings, our weaknesses, and many other things that shape us into who we are, we're more likely to be convinced that there is no God at all."

"I do believe God exists," I clarify with a certain tinge of defensiveness, "it just seems like He's kind of oblivious to what's going on here around us."

"My friend, God has already convinced me of his great love for the human race."

"He convinced you? And how did He do that?"

"I can't tell you. You have to discover that by yourself."

"Come on, man."

"You'll understand in due time, my friend," he finishes with a little smile.

I really like this guy because he hasn't quoted any Scriptures on me. Most of the men that turn to God behind bars are a bunch of hypocrites; they do so thinking that God is going to reduce their sentence, or that a mighty force out of nowhere will suddenly appear and take them out of prison. Their faith is always conditional; when everything is going well, when they have good health, and family and friends write to them or come to visit, everything is caused by the God who is love, but when things look like hell, they immediately drop the Bible, assuring and complaining within themselves that God has abandoned them. They simply seek

God as a means to satisfy their needs. Manu seems to be different. I haven't seen him walking around condemning people with a Sacred Book in hand.

Lunch time is over. My cellie and I take refuge in our bunks as the rest prefers to wander around the jungle of the day room. We sleep for a while. Then I wake up, a bit moody, like a kid who doesn't really know why. I think my cellie has a class this afternoon but he doesn't seem to remember. I sit on the toilet, and the flush seems to crush Manu's profound sleep, but he refuses to be awaken, groaning quietly like a baby. The damn air gets trapped in here; it never moves. It smells really bad all the time. I feel sorry for my cellie.

"Hey, bro," Manu whispers a bit fuzzily. "Whatcha doing?" My face erupts in a huge smirk as my cellie covers his nose, realizing I have just used the toilet. We both laugh.

"Don't you have a class, bro? I ask.

"Yeah, right after the count." Manu sits on the edge of his bunk while I pull off my shirt and throw myself on the floor for some push-ups. He grabs a book and leafs through it as if trying to find something. Then he gets off his bed to reach for his yellow envelope, pulls out a few photographs, and then contemplates them with nostalgia, putting each on different sections.

When I finish my workout, I lie on my bunk and dry off the sweat from my face and chest with a towel, breathing heavily as I sadly contemplate a few photographs of my little girl and wife taped on the bottom of my cellie's bunk.

About an hour later, the four o'clock count is announced and we all stand by the door. When it clears, my cellie takes his books and goes off to class while I remain in the cell. Alone. But this time I begin to consider, though reluctantly, what Manu shared with me about such emotional turmoil.

At dinner, Manu joins up again. I'm used to having him around now. He sits once again in front of me; he bows his head to pray before his meal, and then begins to speak with excitement. "You know, we had a great class today. Father Joe Lopez talked to us about the Ten Commandments in a very interesting way. He said we…"

"Oh, come on, man," I interrupt insolently, "Pray for your fellow prisoners; Never judge anyone; Be aware of the power of your word…Manu those things are impossible to do behind these fences."

Manu looks at me suspiciously, confused with my constant behavior change. His baffled silence and facial expression make me realize he isn't talking about the Ten Prison Commandments found on the letter I snatched from his property while he was away. He's referring to the actual Ten Commandments of the Bible! I feel ashamed, without anything else to say.

"Michael, that's something a bit different," he states calmly. "I'm in fact talking about the commandments in the Bible. And, yes, you're right in a sense, but not quite. I mean, I don't think it's impossible to live out the commandments behind these walls; difficult, yes, impossible, no."

Something tells me he knows about my intrusion with his property, but he doesn't seem to mind. I remain speechless for a little while, listening to the babbling of countless inmates, which seems to multiply the density of my inner anxiety.

"What's up, brothers!" yells Eddie from a nearby table. Manu and I turn to acknowledge his greeting, which is followed by a cordial facial gesture from the rest of the guys sitting with him. "You're more than welcome to join us for prayer and reflection after dinner!" he continues screaming, "Seriously, God's been waiting for ya'll."

Some of the men sitting at our table look angrily at Eddie but he pays no heed; he simply smiles at them.

"So what do you say?" Manu inquires, taking a sip of water. I want to say no but deep inside something tells me to give it a try. I think about it for a moment before responding with a yes. Manu grins and gently caresses my head.

When dinner is over we march back to the unit, but on the way there, a couple of guards separate my cellie and I from the rest, taking us to a nasty, tiny cell. We remain there patiently for a few hours, wondering why, of all the prisoners, it had to be us. Suddenly, the sound of a key rattling in the lock interrupts my thoughts.

"Strip naked!" one of the guards huffs angrily.

"What's the problem?" I exclaim. "What for?"

"Strip naked," another guard repeats more calmly. My cellie seems to be accustomed to this dehumanizing, degrading routine, but not me.

"I ain't takin' my clothes off," I complain. But my cellie does begin to remove, though hesitantly, his white jumpsuit, placing it carefully on a chair as if it was made of fine, delicate fabric.

"Turn around and bend over!" the huge, angry guard demands. Emmanuel's human dignity seems to shrink with such a command, but follows the officer's directions.

"Come on, ladies, we ain't got the whole day."

I resolve to comply, with disdain and pent up fury.

After the strip search, we are led back to the unit with our hands cuffed and our souls mutilated.

Eddie and his friends are clustered around the same spot and stare at us with an inviting look. Manu smiles sadly and rushes to the cell. Then he comes back out with a Bible stuck under his right arm. As I walk towards the religious guys' table, Necio stands in the way shaking his head and pursing his lips.

"It's your last chance, *ese*," he mutters, clenching his fists. "You know I ain't playing games," he threatens as he moves out of my way.

The men on the table gaze at me compassionately while Eddie stands to offer me his bench. There are seven of us gathered around the table which can only sit four men. Manu remains standing by Eddie's side as if to help lead the reflection.

"Alright, my brothers," begins Eddie with a cheerful voice. "First of all, let's welcome our brother Michael with a big round of applause." Everyone follows Eddie's instruction which makes me turn red, blue, yellow, and who knows how many other colors. Some of the prisoners sitting at other tables, and even those watching TV, turn around to witness the embarrassing scene, which makes me hang my head and look at the floor. Eddie notices my discomfort and invites the guys to introduce themselves so I can be more at ease. Although I know most of them by their nickname, their formal introduction does in fact make me feel a bit more comfortable.

Then Eddie takes over again. "This evening we're gonna talk about God," he grins, dimples appearing on his fat cheeks. The guys chuckle. "No, seriously, I'd like to talk about the handout I gave you yesterday, about the Ten Prison Commandments. I hope ya'll had a chance to look at them and reflect upon them."

Manu turns to me and smiles. I try to smile back but I can't.

"Like I said to you yesterday, we're gonna discuss these commandments and try to put them into practice the best we can. So let's see, what's the first one?"

"PRAY FOR YOUR FELLOW PRISONERS, ALL OF THEM," Ricky, a short, chubby guy responds quickly.

"Okay, and what do you all think about it?"

"I think that as Christians," explains Grandpa sitting next to me, "that is our first responsibility: to pray and to reach out to others, regardless of who they are. It's hard to do sometimes but we should never stop trying."

"Thank you Mr. Johnson," Eddie says, "that's very true, challenging but true. It's very easy for a person to pray for those he loves, for the good neighbor; but how often do we take some time to pray for those we don't get along with?"

"It's indeed difficult," Grandpa replies again, eager to share his wisdom, "but it's precisely there, through our intercession for our enemies, that our love for God is best demonstrated. And some of you might wonder: who is my enemy? It's important to understand that the men around us are not our enemies but individuals trying to survive in an unnatural setting.

"After being in the pen for many years now, I've noticed that most of the prisoners, whether they show it or not, are full of fear and come from broken families. These are men like you and me, with deep wounds in their hearts, scars, and usually, so to speak, with a damaged programming in their emotional wiring. The abuse from the penal system, the isolation from their families and friends, and the scorn of society are like poisonous daggers thrust into the prisoner's heart. For that reason, the prisoner tends to glance at everything with suspicion. But if we as Christians do our best in showing them respect, understanding, solidarity, but most importantly, if we could just pray sincerely for one another, the whole environment would be different."

"Come on, man," I protest once again, but this time more respectfully, against his sissy, pious, and impractical solution to the harsh reality around us. They all turn to me but I don't hold back and express myself, "that's just, I don't know, nonsense. It's impossible to do that around here. Are you guys crazy? Have you listened to yourselves?"

"When I talked about showing understanding and solidarity," Grandpa defends himself with unbelievable calmness, "I meant that all of us are struggling with very similar emotions and concerns. How do you think I've managed to survive all these years enmeshed in this madness?

The key has always been about respect and a spirit of solidarity."

"Alright," I exclaim, unable to conceal my strong disagreement, "so what if someone comes up to me, yelling at me all kinds of crap; am I supposed to just stand there and let him scream all he wants without saying anything?"

"Some people believe, Michael," Eddie takes up eloquently, "that remaining silent before your aggressor is a sign of weakness. But many times silence is your best weapon."

"Not only that," the old man expresses, "if you take a look at the Prison Commandments, there's one that invites you to make use of your word wisely. Your word has the power to edify, to build, or the power to destroy. You choose. If you respond with respect and compassion, you're not only saving yourself from the prison drama, you're also helping your aggressor realize that real friendships can take place and that not everyone is out there to get them. We cannot control the attitude and behavior of others, but we do have control over our reactions."

"Yo, niggas," shouts Thomas, a tall, skinny black man of about forty years of age. He approaches the table with a smile on his lanky face, perspiring, as if he had been working out. "I'm sorry, my brothers," he states shaking his head, "I completely forgot we had a gathering this evening." Everyone welcomes him clasping his hand. He opens his Bible to pull out the folded handout of the Ten Prison Commandments and gently places the sacred book on the table.

"It's aright," Eddie offers, "we barely startin'." I take advantage of Thomas' late arrival to excuse myself to go to the restroom with a feeling of distress. When I finish, I make my way to the TV area. The religious guys shoot a sad smile at me but don't say anything.

Flaco shows up. "What's up, man," he greets with a pat on my back, "I didn't know you was that religious," he jokes.

I let a quick, deformed smirk show I'm not pleased by his teasing, and he apologizes.

"*Ese*, just came to tell you that fool's staring at you like he's up to something. Watch out, *homito*, they was talkin' to each other and lookin' at you when you was with the *cristianos*[6]. *Ponte trucha.*[7]"

I know they're watching, but I don't want to stab anybody; and yet, if I don't do it, I know very well the fate that awaits me.

"Gotta go, bro," Flaco utters, leaving me with a heavier burden. I close my eyes and remain still for several minutes, trying to gain control of my feelings but I can't. I begin to cry from the abyss of my eyes, but tears refuse to come out. I turn slowly and discreetly to Necio's spot and find him and his crew throwing poisonous darts at me with their eyes. He flashes some gang signs with his hands, raising my adrenaline. Then I stand up and fix my enraged eyes on them as I walk once again towards the nasty restroom area. Necio and two of his men follow me. I glance at the picket but the guard, Martinez, is busy looking with lust at a magazine. I stand in front of the shower stalls while Necio and his followers surround the small area. One of them pretends he's exercising and the other toys with a piece of paper. The rest of the prisoners are immersed in their own bubble, yet some of them know what's about to happen.

"I told you, *ese*, I ain't playin' games," Necio barks, seething through his teeth. His tough appearance is stronger than ever and he knows it, but I show no signs of being scared.

"Consider this a warning, Mikey," he says, with a fake calmness and a huge aura of pride; then he pulls something

---

[6] Christians
[7] watch out

out of his ass. Not literally, of course.

It's a shank.

The other two guys clear their throats with an exaggerated sound, as if to give Necio permission to finish the task. He scrunches his teeth to gather strength to drive the blunt plastic weapon into my skin, but the dramatic scene is suddenly interrupted by Grandpa.

"That's enough," he states calmly, "Let him go."

The men burst out laughing; but Grandpa's personality has presence and authority. I can't help feeling stunned. Necio stiffens as a flurry of wrath rolls over him. He purses his lips and with great arrogance advises the old fellow to stay out of this but he refuses. He looks like an enraged monster that doesn't know who to attack first.

"What do you want, old man? You gonna jump for him or what?" Necio snarls, clutching the shank with all his might, while the old man defies their arrogance and anger, standing right in front of them, completely unafraid.

"Your fists won't defend you forever, son," Grandpa responds, "When you reach my age and your vigorous strength vanishes, you will realize that it would've been better to spend your time making friends and allies rather than enemies. Those men at your side will sooner or later turn their back on you because their perception of brotherhood is based on the wrong understanding of honor and respect."

"Shut the up!" Necio howls as if Grandpa's words had struck his machismo with an incredible force.

"Please let him go," he implores again. Necio locks his gaze into Grandpa's, slowly losing his mind. Then he gives in with great reluctance, barking at me again, with his jaw clenched in anger, "Get outta here!"

Feeling relentless contempt, I observe his cynical attitude, then I sneer at him as I leave, adding more fuel to the flame of his fury. Grandpa stays with them, and in a matter of seconds, Necio seizes him by the neck and bumps his head against the filthy wall. One of the other men quickly delivers a kick in his stomach, knocking the wind out of him. He falls to the ground like a sack of potatoes while receiving mercilessly kicks and punches all over his feeble body. My heart beats so fast it almost gets out of my chest. I begin to sob silently in the depths of my heart when I notice that Grandpa isn't moving. The final impact he received on his head knocked him out. I want to shout my frustration with a scream but I hold back. Necio and his crew pass right in front of me howling, with evil expressions on their faces. I feel the rage and hatred running through my veins as I lower my head and bite my right fist to quench the feelings.

"Michael!" Manu cries out with unbridled desperation. "What happened in there? Where's Grandpa?" I want to explain what has just happened but a knot in my throat blocks my words. I point at the area with my chin and Manu immediately heads in that direction. The rest of the Bible group looks at me with tender, sorrowful eyes. Eddie shakes his head in disapproval, then comes up to me.

"Please, bro," he tells me, putting his hand on my back, "don't let this prison drama drag you down; don't let it destroy you."

I gaze at him with a confused grimace which then mutates into a cry for help. Officer Martinez announces it's time to rack up, which provokes a grisly anxiety to fall over me. I feel as if a ghost is squeezing my throat. Everyone obeys the guard's order like programmed robots while I turn around to make sure Grandpa is awake. I walk fast towards the restroom, dodging the stampede of prisoners marching back to their caves. I find Eddie and Manu wiping the old man's face covered in blood. They gently probe around the soggy gash while Grandpa tries to sustain his body with his fragile legs. And as they do this, I feel a rampant rush of guilt sweep over me. Grandpa moans a bit, struggling to conceal his profound pain. He staggers towards me, trying to draw a smile but fails. Martinez observes with indifference the old fellow's deformed appearance from his safety glass box and immediately curses at us to leave him there, remarking that medical staff will come to assist him. They do show up, to my surprise, after some twenty minutes, taking Grandpa to the infirmary. I watch with remorse their dramatic departure through the small window, from inside my cell. Everyone does the same.

CHAPTER FOUR

I toss and turn in bed, unable to sleep. Manu remains frozen on his bunk, sadly leafing through his Bible. I have a strange feeling. Memories begin to invade my head to the point of causing me distress. I think about the many mistakes I've made and the things that continue to hurt me deep inside. I feel enraged and an unrelenting desire for revenge.

The cell feels colder as the night slowly fades away. I sense the shadow of death sitting next to me. I get up and pace back and forth, breaking out in a cold sweat. I peek through the glass to look at the sky, which is filled with pale, tiny stars. The moon has slipped out of sight.

"God, what's wrong with me?" I murmur, rubbing my face harshly with both hands. A few tears involuntarily escape and pave their way down my cheeks. It's past midnight and I'm not able to sleep at all. I sit on the floor and stare at the ceiling for a while, hoping the clutter of memories and the bizarre mixture of emotions will stop battling within me. Suddenly, the sound of Manu's gentle snoring fills the cell. I smile sadly. Although I try to give the appearance of indifference and toughness with my cellie and the religious guys, the truth is that their kind gestures have moved my deepest feelings, making me believe in the possibility of experiencing true peace of heart and mind behind these fences. I turn to stare at the dim light for a while, then I close my eyes.

It's already morning. Manu's attempt to get off the bunk as he whistles like an ugly bird wakes me up.

"Morning, cellie," I whisper sluggishly.

"Morning, *vato loco*," he replies, snatching my blankets playfully. "Time to get up."

"What the heck, man," I complain like a kid, twitching my body, "it's cold, give 'em back." Manu laughs and then apologizes, throwing the sheets back at me. I wrap myself around them while he sits on the toilet, sighing.

The intercom suddenly announces the code that congregates the squadron to kick the asses of the rebels in a unit nearby. I cover my head, dismissing the idea of getting out of bed any time soon. A dark dungeon of frustration seems to confine my mind again in the underworld of the prison.

Oh, God, will I ever be able to see my loved ones again? When will this nightmare come to an end? Please, don't let me die in this madness. Who will remember me if I die here?

"Mikey?" my cellie articulates with a soft voice, liberating me from the shackles of my thoughts, "if you're gonna go out there, please, be careful, man. Don't get in trouble."

"It's aright, bro. I'm not going anywhere."

"I went to commissary yesterday and bought quite a few things; we can make some lunch here if you want."

"Yeah, sounds good," I mutter.

Manu walks to the door and glimpses through the glass to see if the Christian brothers are gathered in their usual area.

"Homie," my cellie exclaims.

"Wuz up," I grunt.

"I wanted to ask you something, if you don't mind."

"What is it?" I respond, tossing again to face him.

"Why did you leave the table yesterday? Was it something we said that bothered you?"

I remain silent for a little while.

"No, homie, it's just that… all these things you and the others talk about… I mean, it's all new to me. It's a really challenging way of looking at life, you know; I don't know what to believe."

"*Homito*, I'd just encourage you to be patient with God and with yourself."

His advice automatically traces an awful question mark all over my face, but he quickly speaks to clarify. "Look, being patient with yourself and God are part of the Ten Prison Commandments for a reason. Many prisoners easily give up on God when their prayer is not answered in their own way and time, but, believe me, God responds to every single cry for help, but it takes patience and faith to gradually discover that our spiritual requests are not ignored. If we were to look at the bigger picture of our life, we would immediately identify the times when God intervened in our lives, rescuing us at times even from ourselves. Right at the moment nothing seems to make sense, but if we hold on to our faith in Him in good times and in bad, things will become clearer to us. Understand this, bro, faith means waiting patiently and humbly. As you grow spiritually, as you mature in your faith, you will one day realize that faith in God doesn't make things any easier or any faster, but it does make them possible."

"Look," I utter, with an edge of toughness in my voice, "I know God has me here for a reason…"

"Michael," my cellie interrupts, "God doesn't 'have you' here because He wants to. You know full well He didn't put you in here in the first place. You and I know very well that every single action carries a reaction. Although I do believe there are some prisoners here that are innocent and are simply paying the price of a corrupt criminal system, the majority of us are suffering the consequences of our actions. You know what you did or didn't do, so don't try to disguise your own faults as God's plan for your life. God wants you to be happy in all aspects of your being; that's his plan. What happens is that our arrogance and selfishness make us believe that our plan is much better than God's, and that's when things begin to crumble. Understand this, my friend, life will always give you back whatever you give out. The consequences of any of your actions will sooner or later come knocking on your door. It's not God, it's the choices you made that brought you here."

I gulp and sigh heavily as I hide my face in my hands, knowing deep inside that what he said is true.

"Michael," my cellie speaks again, "Open the eyes of your soul to see beyond these walls, beyond the endless coils of razor wire. Have the courage to tear down the walls of your pride. Dare to open the iron doors that have your soul in solitary confinement. You know who has the key to those doors."

He finishes with a friendly and compassionate smile.

My cellie's words echo in the abyss of my heart as an invisible force begs me to take this opportunity to pour out the poison stored in my bitter soul, but my pride and an inexplicable disgust to appear weak and vulnerable before him prevents me from doing so. Manu sits on his haunches, extends his right hand and places it on my shoulder. I tense up.

"Michael," he whispers, staring at a small bleeding heart tattooed on my arm, "it's okay, things will get better one day. Just have a little faith."

"Thanks, man." I sit up and recline on the wall, closing my eyes as if to transport myself back in time. A huge flood of memories suddenly alienate me from reality. Then a lacerating anguish begins to suffocate me.

"Look, Manu," I state a bit bashfully, "I really wanna do something with my life, bro, but I need someone to help me. I've been a loner all my life. Been through a lot of hell."

Manu looks at me with a tenderness I haven't seen in anybody before. His glowing eyes tell me I can trust in him. I break down.

"I'm here for you, my friend," he manifests firmly, wrapping his arm around my back. I close my eyes again in an attempt to dig out those painful, putrefied memories that have been festering my heart and tormenting my existence, but my words come out empty.

"It's alright, homeboy, just know I'm here." He stands up and leans against the door, then solemnly crosses his arms. A few minutes later, he excuses himself to go check on Grandpa while I grab my towel to take a shower.

"Yo, nigga, wuz up," Thomas yells with exaggerated amazement as he sees me appear in the day room. Eddie stands by his side, gazing at me with a look that begs for an explanation. Other prisoners glance at me with contempt, especially Necio's mob which sits together in the same place, close to the TV area, plotting their next move.

"Come on over, bro. Sit down with us." I obey Thomas' request and immediately Ricky, Tony, and another guy named Roger, approach the table. Manu arrives a little later and sits next to me; Eddie drops his weight to my left and the rest remain standing around like bodyguards.

"Look," I begin lowering my head, "I'm sorry. I know it's my fault."

"Hey, brother," Eddie interrupts, "we're not here to judge you; we're here cuz we wanna help you. But we do wanna know what happened last night."

I remain silent.

"Brother," Eddie states once again with his peculiar diction while getting closer to me, "if you don't wanna talk right now, it's fine, just remember we're here for you."

His words sound sincere but I'm still suspicious about trusting all of these men. Is this even real? Can this type of friendship and brotherhood actually take place in an environment like this? I doubt it.

"Look, homeboy," Ricky speaks, placing his hand on my shoulder. "I understand how difficult this is for you," he states as if guessing what's going on within me, "Most of us are so used to being treated like trash all the time. Prison has the power to destroy your hope, faith, love, trust, and anything inside of you. I know you can't just open up to anybody and be able to reveal your emotions or whatever is going on in your heart. A lot of men around here think we're a bunch of hypocrites, but I don't care. Some individuals don't understand that people do change through the Grace, Love and Mercy of God. Most of us, if not all, have the desire to change our lives, but not many have the courage to do so because they see it as a weakness. We have made it our mission to encourage each other, to follow the commandment to love one another. We don't just want it to be 'a desire for change,' we want that desire to be fulfilled. I know it's difficult to believe, but give yourself the opportunity to be loved and to offer the love you have to others. You're a good man, Michael. Trust in God. Believe in yourself," he remarks, squeezing the back of my neck.

A couple of tears begin to form in the depths of my eyes but I dry them off with the toughness of my heart. They all look at me with a great desire to help me.

"Sorry, but I just can't," I exclaim, rubbing my eyes with both hands. "I'm so pissed right now. That fool is gonna pay for what he did to Grandpa."

"Take it easy, my brother," interrupts Thomas with calmness. "You need to learn to control your anger, or you're gonna end up goin' crazy, or buried six feet under the ground."

"I know, but it's just that sometimes these motherfu…"

"The problem is…" Eddie states, then suddenly stops himself in the middle of his sentence as if he's just seen a ghost. I turn around and it's Grandpa walking this way. We're all surprised. His bruised lips attempt to smile but fail. The entire unit fixes their eyes on him.

I get up to allow him to sit down. He grips my arm to help himself sustain his weight as he delicately sits himself on the bench.

"I can't believe you're already starting without me," he mumbles playfully.

"I'll be right back," says Thomas as he leaves in a hurry.

"How you feeling, Grandpa?" Tony asks.

"I'm doing alright, thanks. But we're not here to talk about me, are we? We gather to talk about the boss: G.O.D.," he finishes with a deformed smile, then a wince.

"Our brother Michael was sharing something before you got here," Eddie informs, and they all turn to me.

"What was that about?" Grandpa stammers.

"Nothing, really. I was just telling them how powerless and angry I feel. I wish I could blow their heads up right now. I never thought they'd do something like that to you."

I lower my head to contemplate the tattoos on my forearms as the others, like members of a jury, wait for me to say more.

Silence takes over for a moment. Then Grandpa speaks softly and with difficulty, "Getting revenge, my boy, will only make things worse. There is no point in fighting violence with violence. Being angry is okay, it's a human reaction to something that makes us feel uncomfortable. But you need to be careful, don't let it control you."

"Sorry, homeboys," I utter, "but every time I see that idiot I feel like…"

"Look, Michael," grandpa slowly articulates, clearing his throat, "forget for a moment about the incident last night, and think about the things that make you angry. If you think about it, most of our anger is caused because things around here are not the way we want them to be. We think we know how prison should be run and how others ought to behave around us. We want to be in control of this prison reality, of the events that take place in the unit. We're pretty much selfish human beings. And, so, here's the challenge: we have to be masters of our anger and not slaves; we need to be in control of our own reality. If we create peace and harmony within our own worlds, it'll be easier to bring it to others."

Manu breaks in, "It's also important to stress that we begin with our own self because we hold absolutely no power to control the events around us. You have no control over people's emotions and reactions towards a specific event or situation, but you do have control over your own behavior. You can choose how to react to something."

"That's right," Grandpa adds, "you can choose to react with violence or you can choose to react with respect and compassion. If you do the latter, you will discover that your aggressor does not persecute you because of who you are but because of who he is. His reality, his world may not be in harmony with himself, God, and much less with the rest of humanity. The physical or verbal violence he's using to hurt you are only a reflection of his own world, not yours. So, once again, you don't have the power to control his feelings or events in his world, but you do hold the power to control your behavior and choose your reaction."

"There are two important words I always pay attention to as I reflect on my own anger," Tony expands on the subject. "These are key to being able to create peace and harmony in all realities: Understanding and Acceptance. These two terms are rooted in the second commandment, NEVER JUDGE ANYONE. We must understand that people have strengths and weaknesses, goodness and faults. Accepting a person with all of these characteristics will make it easier to create peace within both your world and his."

I press my lips firmly together as if resisting to believe in his concepts, then I run my fingers through my hair.

"Let's put it this way," Tony continues, "if we only knew the history of the other person, if we could only travel inside his life and in the depths of his heart and soul, if we knew all the experiences the person has had with his family and everybody else around him, we would be able to look at the person and be more understanding and accepting."

"You're right," I reply, "but the history and past experiences of the person, either as a child or adolescent, don't give him the right to do whatever he wants. As painful as his past may have been, his behavior, his wrongdoing is not justified."

"We're not talking about justifying anybody's mistakes in life. What we're trying to do here is to learn to understand and accept others as they are. And true acceptance means embracing the other as he is, with kindness and compassion, and most importantly, with the hope that one day a real change of heart can take place. We cannot force change on anybody, but we can at least provide a decent, peaceful and welcoming environment so that such a change of heart can occur."

"Hey, ya'll, I'm back," Thomas screams, placing a bunch of snacks on the table. He holds an instant soup which then hands over to me, leaving me in awe. It tastes really good. I thank Thomas for his kind, unexpected offer.

"Hey, I'm gonna go get some snacks, too," Roger, the introverted of the group, exclaims. In a few minutes, he comes back with quite a few things for all of us. I feel strange. What's all this? These men seem to share everything with one another.

"So what if the person doesn't wanna change?" I ask, savoring my soup.

"No one will force him, it's his decision," Grandpa responds between slow munches, "if he's happy with what he's done and who he is, he doesn't have to. But we're still called to respect and to love him the way he is."

His response bothers me. I know this is something I longed for, to be able to share my deepest feelings with someone, but I'm afraid I'll never be able to accept all this business of love, especially behind these walls. What if they're just pretending to care? I don't know, it just sounds so pious and sissy. I can sense their sincerity, but it's so idealistic and impractical. This is no place for attitudes of that sort. God! I feel utterly disconcerted.

"Sorry," I utter in distress, "it's just that… I mean, it's impossible for me to follow your way of life. It's just not who I am."

"And we respect that, Michael; we accept you as you are," Eddie asserts, "but let me ask you something: are you happy with who you are right now and with what you've done so far in your life?"

His question pierces my heart. I remain mute, rolling my eyes, knowing the answer but refusing to articulate it. The noise and tension of the unit increase my anguish.

Grandpa remarks, "You will never find true happiness, my boy, until your reality is in harmony with God; until your world is able to welcome with love and compassion other peoples' worlds."

I ponder on his words for a moment as I finish my noodle soup with great delight. I wipe my mouth with the towel and utter thanks to all the brothers for their welcoming attitude and sharing. Then I head to the restroom area to take a shower.

"Michael," Manu calls out. "I have a few hygiene items for you in the locker. I noticed you don't have anything left."

I lower my downcast eyes and mumble thanks.

After a quick shower, I go back to the cell. But on my way there, I notice Necio and his clan hurling a piercing glare at me as they gossip among themselves. If looks could kill, I would have fallen as if lighting had struck me. I lie on my bunk for a little while, thinking. I feel something inexplicable happening to me. I can't describe it; all I know is that it gnaws me in a strange way.

A little later, Manu enters the cell and crawls up to his bed. He takes a book and leafs through it, uninterested and troubled.

"What's the matter, cellie?" I query, intrigued.

"Necio came up to us," he answers sadly, "threatening the whole group. He wants us to leave you alone."

A blinding rage begins to run through my veins. It's not fair. Everything is between him and I. Why mess with these righteous men?

"That's it!" I yell at the top of my voice.

"Take it easy, bro; don't worry about it. We'll figure something out."

I breathe heavily, trying to conceal my unbridled fury.

"We're praying for him and his men, Michael; things will be fine. Patience, remember?

"Screw that!" I shout at him with all my strength. "That fool's gonna pay for this!" I get up and rush out of the cave with gusts of wrath flowing through the pores of my skin.

"Michael," Grandpa exclaims between repressed moans upon seeing me appear in the common area, "come over here." I walk towards him with my head held up, tightening my teeth. He's sitting by himself on a bench, holding a religious stamp. "I know what you're feeling right now, so calm down," he advises, sensing the density of my contempt for Necio and his crew.

"We gotta talk, son," he continues, "I know what's going on between the two of you. I believe the whole unit is aware of your rivalry now."

I hang my head, frustrated, refusing to explain myself.

"Michael, you wanna tell me exactly what's going on?

You really thought Necio and his little puppets were your brothers, huh?"

"Look, Grandpa, I appreciate all you do for me, but I don't wanna get you and the others in trouble."

"Michael, that man already came up to us with the warning to leave you alone. I told him we won't; he got pissed and walked away. But I know he's up to something. I need to know what's really going on. What happened, son?"

Grandpa's concern is genuine, loaded with compassion and a real desire to help. I clear my throat as I drop my body on the steel bench in front of him. He fixes the bandage around his head and sighs. The block feels cold and I begin to shiver a little. The rest of the religious guys aren't around so I feel more comfortable unveiling a bit of myself to the old fellow.

"Well," I begin mumbling, "you know the beginning of the story. I used to hang out with them *vatos*; I was part of their so-called brotherhood. But one day I was told to do something I didn't agree with. Something I wasn't expecting. They wanted me to stab that kid over there." I point at Isidro, a young man who grew up in my neighborhood. "He and my little brother used to go to school together, and sometimes they'd come home to play with other kids in the backyard. His mother and my mother were very close friends, so I told Necio why I couldn't do the job but he didn't care, so I just decided to drop out without telling anybody. And as you can see, I'm paying the consequences."

"And what's Necio's problem with that kid?" Grandpa asks.

"Isidro is a kitchen hustler," I explain, "he trades with Necio whatever he steals from the kitchen for marijuana. Or at least they used to, up until, like, two weeks ago."

"Why, what happened?"

"I don't know exactly, but apparently Necio was claiming a debt that Isidro had already paid. Necio stubbornly insisted the money had to be paid or there'd be consequences. But Isidro refused to pay and immediately stopped the trade. The other got pissed, and you know the rest."

"Oh, God," Grandpa sighs, running his fingers through his short, white beard. His lined face denotes preoccupation. "Look, son, I don't know what's on your mind right now, but I can assure you that confronting Necio with violence won't change anything; it'll just make things worse. Let's think about something more mature and peaceful."

Once again I'm annoyed by his pious and absurd solution to a ruthless reality. He knows full well that if we don't respond with violence, the predator will continue to abuse the prey. Why does he keep insisting that we take a nonviolent stance after the beating he received yesterday? We remain silent for a while, mutually waiting for the other to proceed with the conversation.

"Grandpa," I finally declare humbly, "I'm sorry for being so dumb and stubborn. I really wish I could be like you and take things less personally, but it's just the way I am. Don't get me wrong, sometimes I do wish I could do something better with my life. Deep inside I wanna be a better man to my family and those around me but I don't know how. To start with, I need a lot of help with my faith. Sometimes I feel like God has disappeared, or that he's just indifferent to my plea, to my cry for help. I struggle a lot to feel His presence."

"There is absolutely no doubt that you're dumb and stubborn," he jokes, flashing a distorted grin.

I smile sadly.

"No, seriously, my boy, I know what you're talking about. But you must know that our relationship with God, like any other relationship, takes time to grow. At times your intimacy with Him will grow strong, and at other times it will wither. That's why we keep encouraging each other to be patient with ourselves. God is always present, son, but our ability to see him is not always that clear, sometimes is a bit clouded."

"But why? Why is God so mysterious? Why is it so difficult to feel his presence?" I ask, with an odd interest.

"You've heard them say that God is a mystery. Well, God is a mystery as much as our relationship with Him. The problem with us human beings is that we have a hard time accepting God's mysterious nature; it bothers us that we will never be able to understand his ways, and why certain things happen. We're not very good at dealing with mysteries and because of this, we grow tired and impatient. But understand this, my boy, if God were to reveal Himself fully in this life, humans would immediately lose the sense of wonder. We waste a lot of time trying to come up with explanations about the mystery of God, instead of focusing our time and effort to understand that God appears in unexpected opportunities and people."[8]

"It's true, Grandpa, but I don't think my real problem has to do with Him being a mystery," I defend myself, "it's just that I don't know how to relate to him. Sometimes I see him as a close friend, and other times as a distant tyrant who watches with indifference his people suffer."

"We all have our own ideas and perceptions of God," Grandpa states reverently, "but we must understand that the real God is not the same as our ideas of God. God is beyond description. He cannot be captured in words. And sometimes we believe we can fit God into our limited, narrow way of thinking. Let me give you an example, using your own experience of God. Many of us may refer to God as a close, loving friend, and that's a nice image, but God is more than that. When we call Him a 'loving friend,' we already have an idea of how a loving friend should behave, and so we want God to behave according to that idea. In other words, our ideas of God tend to manipulate the real God."

---

[8] Jane Kopas, *Seeking the Hidden God* (Maryknoll, N.Y.: Orbis, 2005).
In her book, Jane offers a profound, excellent theological and spiritual reflection on the hiddenness and images of God, allowing us to see how lovingly near this God is to all of us.

Grandpa pauses as if to give me time to digest what sounds like a riddle.

"Your other image of God, that of a distant tyrant, I believe is experienced by most of us, if not all. Unfortunately we tend to give God such a title according to our feelings at a particular moment in life. For example, we usually describe God as tyrant and indifferent in times of trial and suffering. But when everything is going well, we refer to him again as loving and caring. We must understand that God is more than feelings and ideas."

"I get it. So you're suggesting that all of us are, so to speak, trapped in our own ideas of God?" I ask, sounding more like I'm making a statement.

"That's right. And we have to get rid of the expectations that God should meet our needs. We must allow God to be God," he remarks.

I nod sincerely in agreement, feeling the strike of each word on my hardened heart.

"You said something about God appearing in unexpected opportunities and people. What exactly did you mean by that?" I inquire.

"My boy, God is hidden in the simple and the ordinary, but many times we're so busy looking for the God we think we know that we miss the opportunity to meet the real, living God. If we're not willing to build a relationship with God in connection with the rest of humanity, that relationship won't grow, because it is in our relationship with one another that we may discover the hiddenness and mystery of God."

Although difficult to embrace, Grandpa's words echo in my mind and then sink into the abyss of my heart. I accept the idea that God is a mystery, but I find it so difficult to believe that a God of love and compassion is hidden in each and every one of us.

"So where is sin in all of this?" I question again with the same strange desire to learn, "do you think sin has anything to do with our inability to feel God's presence?"

"That's a good question, son. As you already know, sin is everywhere. It is our sinful nature that clouds the mind and heart, making it more difficult to embrace God's presence, love, compassion, and forgiveness. When sin gets in the way, we're not only fooled to believe that God is far away, we're also poisoned into the idea that He is indifferent to the pain of humanity."

The squeaky sound of the sliding door being opened stifles the noise of the unit, making me and everyone else turn our heads to see who it is. A nicely dressed woman, whom I believe is one of the social workers, and the chaplain, Father Joe, stand by the door speaking with unit officer Serrano. After a brief conversation, the guard shouts my friend Flaco's last name, "Espinosa, to the door." Flaco looks surprised by the visit and hurries to the entrance, tossing a bag of potato chips on the table and wiping his mouth with his khaki shirt as the rest of the men sitting with him scan the woman with lust. The two visitors disappear with Flaco in the long corridor.

"Tell me, can I talk to you," Roger walks by rapping an MC Magic song, with his radio headphones crammed into his ears, "girl, where do you come from? I been looking for you all of my life…"

Grandpa attempts to smile and grabs him by the sleeve. Roger, shy as he is, smiles and removes his headphones.

"Whatcha guys doin'?" he asks hesitantly.

"We're just talking about life, son," Grandpa utters, twisting his back as if trying to crack his bones. The effort makes him groan.

"What kinda things?" Roger inquires. He's probably in his early twenties, Hispanic, medium height.

"Well, things in general. Faith, suffering, God, mistakes. Things we could've done better. And things we can do much better."

"I see," Roger sighs and adopts a meditative posture, giving the impression of needing some help. "Grandpa, I wanted to ask you something," he breaks his own silence. "I been struggling a lot with this. I mean, I'm into the Word and everything, and really try hard to follow the commandments, you know, but it's just difficult to carry on sometimes. How much longer, Grandpa?" His shoulders sag under a slight burden, his brow furrows, and his eyes implore an explanation.

The old fellow doesn't seem to comprehend Roger's restlessness. "How much longer what, my boy?" Grandpa asks, intrigued.

"How much longer do we have to pay for our mistakes? How much longer do we have to endure this oppressive environment?"

Grandpa's eyes light up, sensing with better precision the source of Roger's burden.

"Don't get me wrong," Roger tries to clarify, "I understand I'm paying the price of my previous actions in the free world, but God knows how much I regret having caused pain to others. God knows this time I'm gonna do things better. My change of heart is real and sincere." Roger gulps as if to dissolve a lump that squeezes his throat.

"Look, son," Grandpa states calmly, "first of all I'm glad you believe that your experience, this situation, was not caused by God. You're right in saying that our actions brought us here; but sometimes the consequences of our wrongdoing can last a lifetime. But we believe that God can give us the strength to endure the difficulties we face in the midst of this madness. The sentence has already been established, whether justly or unjustly, and we cannot do anything about it. We must accept our reality as it is and try to make the best out of it."

Roger nods, hangs his head, and allows a few tears to wet his cheeks.

"I guess I'll need to pray even more, huh?" Roger sighs. Then Grandpa continues, "I know you're a very devout person, Roger, but when you pray, don't do what other prisoners do. Don't try to convince God to believe in the repentance and goodness of your heart so that He may miraculously reduce your sentence. When you pray, just be who you are; don't break your head trying to choose the right words or embellish the way you really feel. Try to see prayer as a relationship with God.

"Many prisoners grow tired or impatient with God and with themselves because they complain their prayer is never answered. The reason they feel that way is because they use prayer to manipulate God. They see it as a refuge, as a safe shelter for when things look like hell, but once the storm and difficulty are over, prayer is immediately abandoned. A real prayer, son, makes us reach out to God, not on our own but on his terms; it pulls us away from our worries and anxieties while challenging us at the same time to enter into a new world that is greater than our narrow boundaries of our mind and heart. Prayer, son, is a great adventure because the God with whom we enter into a new relationship is greater than we are and challenges all our ideas and images of Him.[9]

"When I surrendered my life to God, I began to discover that it is in our darkest moments in life that God is closest to us. Please, don't give up. It's true that the system makes us pay a thousand times for our mistakes, treating us like garbage, like heartless human beings; but understand this, my boy, when we have a good relationship with God and others, a prison can be like a palace; a steel bench like a throne; and the storms of life like a sunny weather."

Roger purses his lips, marveled at Grandpa's words, but he doesn't seem to buy into his last words.

"I do believe what you say, but, come on, Grandpa," he

---

[9] Henri J. M. Nouwen, *Reaching out. The Three Movements of the Spiritual Life* (New York: Doubleday, 1975), p. 126.

declares with respect, yet with an air of skepticism, "look at what happened to you yesterday. You really think prison can be like a palace?"

"Look, son, the man who walks with God may lose his life, but he can never lose his soul. You know well I don't go around looking for trouble. I made the choice yesterday to defend someone respectfully, making use of my words wisely. But Necio, in his absurd idea of manhood, chose to attack me physically. I had the power to choose and control my behavior, but I had absolutely no control over Necio's reaction. It's true, I still feel a lot of pain, but, believe me, my soul remains intact."

I squirm with embarrassment, closing my eyes, knowing that the one he defended is me. What he said about manhood is very true. Many of us turn a drizzle into a hurricane just for the sake of defending an erroneous idea of manhood. How stupid and dumb can I be! I lower my head in disappointment with myself. A strange force from within is beginning to challenge the way I see myself and my surroundings.

"Michael, you okay?" Roger asks, interrupting my thoughts.

"Yeah, I'm fine. Sorry, I just…"

Flashbacks of my afflicted mother begin to attack my mind, adding more weight to my remorseful burden. Broken memories of the cruelty with which I treated my mother and my wife begin to suffocate the little peace that had begun to envelop my innermost being. What's happening to me?

"What's wrong, son?" Grandpa inquires.

"I'm aright," I state firmly. They look at me with unbelieving eyes.

"So, anyway," Roger exclaims, dissatisfied but hopeful, "I guess I gotta keep fighting the good fight."

"Keep up that faith, Roger," the old fellow encourages, patting his shoulder, "we must be strong in good times and in bad; if we lose our faith and hope, we lose everything, even the reason for living."

Roger smiles and excuses himself as he puts his headphones around his neck, flashing a peace sign with both hands. Grandpa is about to take up our conversation again but he's interrupted by the slam of the unit's door. Grandpa and I wiggle in our seats as we watch Flaco coming in with his head hanging, his face downcast and pale, and his eyes red and swollen. His rehearsed sloppy walk of a young adolescent seems to have disappeared. He walks normal, sobbing quietly as he makes his way up the stairs; then he stops before entering the cave. He glances around and lowers his eyes to stare at me. I can see his thick, painful tears from down here. His brown, dull eyes beg for a loving embrace; his whole facial appearance screams at us for help but he doesn't say anything. He grips the cold steel of the handrails while gulping deeply, and then turns around to cage himself in the cold and darkness of his cell. The social worker and Father Joe remain at the entrance chatting with Serrano. They both have a serious and a bit troubled look on their faces. Then after an exchange of handshakes with the officer they abandon the place.

Vaquero, Elmo, and Smiley seem to have seen what I saw. They immediately come to me, asking if I noticed Flaco's affliction.

"Of course I did," I respond, "he looked like he was coming back from hell."

"You think you can find out what happened, son?" Grandpa asks me.

"I'll give it a try, but not right now, I don't think it'd be a good time."

They all agree.

CHAPTER FIVE

I go back to my cell and find Manu looking at his pictures. I greet him and apologize for my reaction earlier, then explain what has just happened with Flaco.

"You've been friends with him for some time, what do you know about him? Maybe we can help."

"Well," I begin, trying to remember what he told me some time ago, "one day he had a fight during a visit with his girl, and two weeks later she sent him a letter, ending their relationship and telling him she had another man. He went crazy in his cell and wanted to do something stupid but Brains, his cellie, stopped him."

Manu shakes his head as he stuffs the pictures back in the yellow envelope.

"But that's about it, I really don't know what made him cry like that a while ago."

"It must've been something terrible," Manu states, turning the quietness of the cell into a sepulchral silence. "The chaplain and the social worker together with Flaco? Something's not right here."

Manu and I opt to skip lunch at the chow hall and stay in our cells until the 4 P.M. count, preparing our own meal. When the doors click open, we immediately get out of the cell while the religious men begin to congregate around the usual spot. My feet walk directly to their table as if they had a mind of their own while Manu makes his way to the TV area to greet a few men, then he approaches our the table.

Eddie is the first one to shake my hand with his distinctive eloquence and everyone follows his welcoming attitude. Grandpa takes over, leading everyone in prayer, asking God for strength, and thanking Him for another afternoon. When he's finished, some sit down while others remain standing around the table.

It's strange. Something deep inside me wants to rejoice in their fellowship, but why? As they continue their group sharing, someone interrupts their excitement with a hollow greeting, followed by an exaggerated clearing of his throat.

It's Brains, Flaco's cellmate.

He approaches me hesitantly and tells me something that pierces my tough attitude, leaving me vulnerable before everyone.

"Flaco hasn't stopped crying since he had that visit with the chaplain and that lady," Brains explains with sympathy. "I think you might be able to help him, since you're one of the closest friends he has in the unit."

His request seems to multiply the weight of my burden as the others look at me with affection, expecting me to say yes.

"What did they tell him, do you know?" I ask Brains. His face turns a bit disconcerted as he tries to avoid the question but the abnormal scratching of his head doesn't lie; there is something deeply wrong going on.

Brains wavers a little.

"We need to know what's going on so we can help," Tony expresses.

Brains sighs, "They told him his parents had a car accident yesterday. His father was killed instantly and his mother is in a comma. The doctors said she won't make it."

Everyone is shocked and a horrible silence among us

takes over. Despair enters through the pores of the brick walls and fuses with the hellish auras of indifference and scorn. Manu hangs his head sadly in disbelief and invites the group to pray for Flaco and his family. We all join hands in the midst of our powerlessness.

"I'll go talk to him after dinner," I mumble after the prayer, then everyone breaks off.

Grandpa is taken to the infirmary for a check-up. Tony and Roger attend an afternoon class. Thomas and Eddie, who both take a correspondence course, sit down to finish their homework. Manu goes back to the cell while I remain standing here, with a million thoughts swirling around in my head.

I sit down to watch TV for some time, uninterested and bored. I close my eyes tightly and begin to consider more seriously everything I've heard so far with the religious men. Is it really possible to experience a true peace of mind and heart behind these evil walls? Is it possible to feel the presence of God in this madness? Can God be discovered in all of us? A wave of tension sweeps over me as the static air that fills the block becomes thicker and struggles to enter into my already congested nostrils. I shake the thoughts off my head, get up and trudge back to my cell with a horrible headache.

I find Manu taking a nap, so I collapse on my bunk to do the same. Sometime later, officer Martinez announces it's time for dinner, and, as always, we gather around the entrance to stroll to the ominous environment of the chow hall.

I sit with Manu and Grandpa. There is something about these men that makes me feel comfortable. I nibble at the food in front of me, annoyed by the deafening chaos of the inmates, which is increased by the barks and heavy steps of the guards walking around like gigantic pit bulls.

Before the meal is over, two white men approach our table and sit on their haunches, close to Grandpa. They exchange a secretive conversation while I try to listen, but the havoc around us weakens the mumbling sounds of the two men. I can only hear Grandpa thanking them for God knows what. When the two inmates leave, the old fellow shakes his head as in disagreement and immediately explains to us their intentions.

"They offered me revenge against Necio and his men, but they wanted my consent. I thanked them for their concern, but I said no, that's not how I fix things."

I spark a half a smile as my admiration for Grandpa and his way of life grows stronger. Manu puts his hand around him and squeezes him a little, making him groan, then chuckle.

"Grandpa," I utter in a serious tone, leaning forward so he can hear me, "I really wish I could make decisions like yours."

Manu looks at me with affection and compassion. He kicks my leg from under the table and then rubs his foot against mine.

"My boy," Grandpa begins as he swallows a piece of thick-plastic-looking meat, "we've talked about this before, about choosing our behavior and reaction to something. I understand that many of us were brought up in a family where relationships were broken and the structure was very unstable. Growing up many of us experienced the absence of a father or mother figure. Or we may have seen our parents fighting most of the time. In other words, the hell we experienced as a child certainly has consequences in our lives. We could argue that because of those experiences our reaction to certain situations tends to be violent, that we're simply responding under the influence of the way we were raised. Regardless, you and I know that violence is not the answer. Just as you 'learned' the behavior passed along to you by your parents or family structure, you can also 'relearn' other behaviors, other reactions and options. Dare to challenge the limited options you inherited from your family; dare to learn new alternatives, new ways of relating with others. Sometimes, son, we must challenge our own beliefs in order to bring about change. Once you organize the whole structure of your belief system, the people around you will begin to change as well because they will be impacted by your attitude towards them. I don't know if you remember, but one of the prison commandments encourages you to focus on the here and now. The past cannot be changed, my boy; we must put all our energy in what we do now, today. We can't spend the rest of our existence blaming the family or the system for everything that goes wrong in our lives. We must take responsibility and be honest with ourselves."

I nod several times in agreement while Manu stacks our trays and squeezes my shoulder with encouragement. His words are like bullets, shot with affection, aiming at my arrogance and ridiculous self-pity.

When the command is given, we all stand up and journey back to the unit, then wait for recreation. I didn't see Flaco in the chow hall, he must still be enmeshed in the quicksand of his cell.

After some time, officer Martinez opens the main door for recreation. Flaco is nowhere to be seen. I feel nervous.

"Hey," Manu shouts behind me, "I'm gonna go run a little bit. Are you gonna go talk to Flaco?"

"Yeah, in a minute."

"Good. I hope you can give him some courage. God be with you. I'll see you in a bit, homeboy."

"Thanks, man. Later."

I gaze around but I don't see any of the other religious guys. Flaco must be alone in his cell. "But what am I gonna to say to him?" I whisper to myself as I head to his place on the second level. I knock on his cell door several times but I get no response. The small window has been covered with a piece of paper so I can't see anything. I go back down, straight to the picket, and find the officer on the phone. I tap on the thick glass to get his attention but he stares at me with indifference. He moves his head up and down in roars of laughter, as though someone on the other end of the line were reciting silly jokes to him. He finally motions me to wait, now swirling around in his chair not unlike a young school girl. Then he hangs up the receiver and opens the door.

"Whatcha want?" he demands rudely.

"Sorry to bother you, but I was wondering if you could open cell 30B. I wanted to talk to Espinosa, but he's not responding, sir."

Martinez, aware of Flaco's situation, nods frowning as he searches my friend's ID card in a plastic box. When he finds it, he exclaims growling, "He should be in there!" The correctional officer pushes a button that unlatches Flaco's cell door. I thank him and go back up, but before attempting to open the door, I shout my homeboy's name a few more times, but, again, no response.

I then resolve to pull the door slowly until it has been completely open. I'm paralyzed immediately by what I see. I feel as if a bucket of cold water has been poured over me. My soul seems to abandon my frozen body and my eyes seem to jump out of their sockets in disbelief. I breathe heavily. Then I finally shout, "Flaco!" My scream echoes for seconds in the unit as my friend's lifeless body hangs from the ceiling. He has a rope around his neck and his cold body still swings slightly in the darkness of his cell. The few prisoners that remained in the unit turn to me, astonished and confused. There are no words to describe the depth of the silence that followed my scream. I close the door and run downstairs towards the picket. Martinez immediately realizes what's going on before I even mutter a word with my shattered voice. I drink some water and sit down for a while, gasping and trying hard to withhold my tears. The officer picks up the phone and calls a bunch of medical people and other officials who immediately arrive, taking my friend away on a mat covered with a white linen.

I walk anxiously back to my cell and wait for Manu, feeling again the shadow of death sitting next to me. I fall on my knees to pray but an invisible current of despair rolls over my entire being, making me shudder and stop the prayer. I get up and pace back and forth clumsily, like a J-cat caged in a mental unit.

Several feelings battle within the restlessness of my heart. I feel powerless. How can this happen! Why! I scream and lament in the depths of my being. My homeboy's decision to terminate his life simply proves he had already been dead a long time ago, tortured innumerable times by the indifference and abuse of the system; mutilated by the distance that separated him from his loved ones, and wounded by the contempt and hostility of an unforgiving society.

It wasn't just the tragedy of his parents that made him do this; his burden and sorrow were far heavier. If he had just had someone he could open himself to. Was no one interested enough in him to listen, to pay attention to him? We are, indeed, dead men walking, seeking desperately to free ourselves from the miseries of this world. Flaco found his way.

Manu shows up after a while and immediately asks about the suicide.

"It's true," I utter, trying to quench an unrelenting helplessness attacking my speech, "I saw him hanging there, Michael, in his cell. Alone. Alone, brother."

Manu's brown eyes begin to drown in a river of sadness as he sits close to me, then he places his head on my shoulder. I don't know why but his gesture brings a certain peace within me. Silence reigns in the cell for some time. Manu's closeness allows me to decipher a Bible verse tattooed on his right arm in gothic letters: 'I am the Way, the Truth, and the Life.' I gulp and heavily clear my throat. Then my cellie walks up to his locker and falls on his knees to pray, gripping the metal storage with both hands.

I don't know what to do, I feel like imitating his ritual but I still find it difficult to express myself, to find the right words. "God, give me the strength to follow you," I pray in my head, "give me the courage to leave my past behind and focus on your ways from now on…"

I drag my back to recline against the wall and close my eyes. I lose track of time and feel like I'm floating in another dimension. When I open my eyes, Manu is already up on his bunk, fully asleep. I get up to use the toilet and then back to bed.

The following day, I wake up right before dawn and peek through the window. There seems to be no stars, only the gloomy gray sky still untouched by the rays of the sun. The dingy light that peers through the glass seems more like the onset of night than the beginning of day. A minor headache begins to trouble me, but a strange scent of flowers flowing out of nowhere immediately makes me ignore the pain. I move my head right to left with exaggerated sniffs, trying to locate the source of such a beautiful aroma but I can't.

For a long time, I stand in front of the door, with my nose pressed to the glass. My breathing turns into mist, which then treads down the window like tears. I sigh heavily several times. My cellie half opens his eyes, but sinks back down and drowses again, crushed by the weight of sleep. I look at my long, crooked shadow stretched towards the ceiling as I hear the wind lashing against the unit's windows. I rub my eyes and shuffle to bed, still intrigued by the beautiful smell.

A few hours later, after the sun has finally stained yellow the entire building, I wake up, grab my towel and walk out into the dayroom. I see Manu and some of the guys stationed around the usual table. They each have a small carton of milk, a few tiny boxes of cereal, and some fruits.

"You get here just in time," Manu articulates with a serious smile, "there's a bowl and a spoon, help yourself."

"Thanks," I respond, hanging the towel over my shoulder, "where are the others?" I ask, pouring some cereal into the bowl which I then splash with a bit of milk.

"Tony and Ricky are at the factory," Grandpa responds, "Eddie in the kitchen, and Roger at the library."

"I see."

"Hard working men," he adds.

"Yo, bro," Thomas shouts from across the table, "ya feelin' aright? I mean, after what happened yesterday, man…We're really sorry, brother."

"It's hard to believe, and I feel bad cuz I know I could've done more to help him. He didn't deserve to die like that."

"We all wish we could've done something more, son," Grandpa states with an aura of sadness, "none of us should end up like that; that's why we must keep encouraging each other, and do our best in building a community of support where everyone is welcome."

"We're all working on that, Grandpa," Manu intervenes, "Right, Michael?"

I smile sadly and simply nod, putting my bowl on the table and getting ready to leave. I thank them for their kindness and acceptance.

"Michael," the old fellow exclaims before I leave, "I wanted to ask you something."

He seems to feel a little better. The bruises on his face are beginning to vanish but he still has that heavy bandage around his head.

"What is it?" I reply.

"It's just an invitation; you don't have to respond right now. I've been a tutor for quite a few years in different academic courses; as you may already know, in all these years in prison I've earned a bachelor's and a master's degree in fine arts, and completed some other spirituality programs that have given my life a purpose, a reason for living. I know I will never see the other side of the world, but I've found my vocation behind these walls. Part of that vocation is helping others diminish their struggles and sufferings during their stay here. But not only that, I also want people to find their own place, their own vocation in life even in the midst of this madness."

Grandpa's words are sincere and his glimmering eyes confirm such honesty, but I still don't know exactly where he's going with this. He places his elbows on the table and looks at Thomas and Manu as if to gather support to articulate his request.

"Look, there is a few universities that offer courses through correspondence; I was wondering if you'd be interested in signing up for some courses. I have all the time in the world, son, so I could give you some guidance."

His request leaves me tongue-tied for seconds.

"What?" I finally exclaim, giggling. "Come on, Grandpa, I'm too old for that."

"Old? Come on, son."

"Michael," Manu interferes, "like Grandpa said, you don't have to decide right now. Just promise you'll really give it some thought."

"I promise," I smile, skeptically, burying my face in my hands. I thank them once again as I walk away to the shower stalls.

Later in the afternoon, right after the odyssey in the chow hall for lunch, I meet up with Grandpa again for an answer. Even though I still can't fully understand the reason behind their generosity, I've decided to take advantage of the opportunities that life, or maybe God, has presented before me through these men. Besides, I'll be spending the next fifteen years in confinement, so why not do something fruitful after all. I don't know why but I have begun to trust these men and even to feel a certain affection for them.

"Grandpa," I begin timidly, searching within myself for a way to begin, "I thought about your help with school. But I was wondering about the cost; I know these courses ain't offered for free."

"I know, son, but I don't want you to worry about that; you leave that to me."

Jesus, I like this guy. There's never a trait of fakeness in his attitude.

"Thanks, Mr. Johnson. I really don't know how to pay you back for everything you do for me."

"Just two things, my boy," he points out erecting two fingers, "one, call me Grandpa, and two, please, no one's talking about paying back, okay? When you do things for others without expecting anything in return, God blesses you even more. But there's certainly something you can do for me."

He smiles.

"What is it?" I reply, hesitantly.

"Do something with your life, son. You don't belong in this hell."

I gulp a couple of times as I glance around the unit. I grasp the back of Grandpa's head, with a strong desire to hug him, but I refrain myself. He grins and then coughs as if he knew of my intention.

"I'm gonna show you the brochure of a university and the degrees offered through correspondence. Then you can decide which route you wanna take."

We both walk up to his cell but before we enter we're immediately paralyzed by the strident sound of the intercom which orders that we drop to the floor with our face down and our hands in the back of the head. It's a shakedown.

An army of uniformed men invades the compound with truncheons attached to their waist and thick plastic shields glued to their forearms. They enter each of the cells with extreme caution as though it is unknown territory for them, sifting through everyone's property to make sure no one is storing any contraband or any other object that might suggest danger to the population or threat to the security. They confiscate a few tiny shanks, small quantities of marihuana, hooch, and even pornographic material.

After about an hour or so, the troops abandon the place, leaving a complete chaos in everyone's cells. I help Grandpa get on his feet and then excuse myself to go to my room.

"I'll meet you at the table in a few minutes with the brochure," he tells me.

"Yeah, I'll see you there."

When I enter the cell, I find Manu picking up a clutter of books and crumpled papers spread all over the floor. The mattresses and sheets were removed and left in total disaster. I fix them at once and then fall to the ground to help my cellie organize his property.

"Good Lord, look at this mess!" I state as I collect a few books and magazines, placing them in the locker. Then without meaning to, I pick up his yellow envelope and give it to him.

"Why do you keep those things in there?" I ask him as he neatly stacks the packet under his books.

"What things?"

"Those old pieces of newspaper, and those blurred photos."

"Have you looked at them?"

"No."

He remains silent. I look at him with a confused grimace.

When everything is in order, my cellie grabs a few snacks for him and hands some over to me. We sit down and eat in the quietness of the cell while some of the men out in the day room still grumble about the intrusion of the squad.

"Hey, homie," I break the silence, "I told Grandpa I'm gonna give school a shot, see what happens."

"You serious?" Manu exclaims with excitement, "man, it's good to hear that."

"Yeah, he said not to worry about the cost, so why not. I just don't understand, though, where's he gonna get the money to pay for the expenses?"

"You should've asked him."

"I kinda did but he said it's not a problem."

"Well, then don't worry about it," he advises calmly as he washes his hands in the sink and spatters some water on his face.

"I'll be back, I told Grandpa I'd meet him at the table for the school info."

"Michael," my cellie calls out as he dries his face off, "I'm proud of you."

"Thanks, man," I reply, almost inaudibly, with a little embarrassment. "Oh, by the way, bro, I wanted to ask you: did you smell anything this morning when you got up?"

"Anything like what? I swear I didn't use the toilet."

I chuckle.

"No, it was something sweet, like roses... I don't know, I might've just dreamed."

"Nope."

"Alright, then. I'll see you in a bit."

"Hey there," Grandpa greets me with a serious and somewhat discouraged tone, holding the brochure.

"You aright?" I ask, dropping my body on the bench.

"Yeah, I'm fine. Necio just came by, with another warning to leave you alone."

My blood begins to boil, but Grandpa seizes my arm gently, trying to calm me down.

"Listen to me, son. It's okay, I can take it. Come on, breathe in and out, control yourself."

"I'm sorry, it's just... God!"

"Patience my boy. Come on, let's say a little prayer for

that man."

I look at Grandpa with astonishment, still with pangs of disagreement about his attitude deep inside, but willing to follow his praying posture.

When he finishes, he opens the brochure and explains in full detail every single degree offered by the university.

When I was a little boy I used to play with my cousins and other kids at our house, writing and scratching the walls with colored pieces of chalk, pretending I was a prominent professor giving a lecture at a prestigious school.

"What's so funny?" Grandpa asks when my face projects a smile.

"I was just remembering when I was a kid I wanted to be a teacher."

"Well, there you go, son; this could be the beginning of a dream."

I sigh with optimism.

"I'm gonna send a formal letter to this university," he points out, "requesting all the paper work to make sure you're enrolled as soon as possible."

"Thank you, Mr. Johnson. I mean, Grandpa."

"Don't mention it, my boy."

"What up, people," Eddie arrives, shouting, greeting the two of us with an elaborate hand shake, "man I had a lotta fun at work. God is good, fellas."

"It's good to see you smiling, son," Grandpa says and then motions him to sit down.

"Where's the rest of the brotherhood? We meeting this afternoon?" Eddie inquires.

"Yes, we are," Grandpa responds, "in fact, Manu volunteered to lead the reflection. Tony and Roger are bringing some snacks, and I have some goodies to share."

"So is our brother here joining us?" Eddie asks, referring to me, of course, with such an enthusiasm that it's hard to say no.

"I sure am," I answer.

"I'll see you later then; I'm gonna take a shower and clean up that mess; I heard about the shakedown."

CHAPTER SIX

After the four o'clock count, the men assemble again in the same area, and with great joy they come bringing all kinds of things to share with one another. They place instant soups on the table, candy bars, and other snacks.

"Come on, brother," Thomas tells me, "don't just look at 'em, help yourself."

"Aright, aright," I respond, throwing my hands at a soup and some potato chips. Eddie offers me his seat, close to Grandpa. Ricky sits right in front of me, smiling graciously with his fat lips. Manu is about to begin the reflection when all of a sudden two prisoners show up.

The chaos and loud noise in the unit seem to be muffled by their appearance, which leaves us all immediately astonished. It's Big Bear and Brains.

"What the…" I murmur to myself as I swallow a portion of my soup.

"Hey brothers," Eddie screams with great delight, "How you doin'?"

Big Bear and Brains look at each other as if to gather courage to state their intentions but stutter.

"What are you looking for?" Manu asks with his typical peaceful character, fueling the men with the energy to speak.

"We'd like to be part of your brotherhood," Big Bear finally decides to speak with a tough diction and gangster mannerisms.

"Of course, of course," Eddie declares passionately, "You're more than welcome."

All of us introduce ourselves to the newcomers and then allow them to share a bit of their background. Brains and Big Bear's reaction is one of amazement as they witness the affection and respect with which we treat each other. Other nearby tables still pitch spears of suspicion with their eyes at us, but the men don't seem to mind.

At the other end of the unit, Elmo, Vaquero, and Smiley are immersed in a swamp of sadness for our friend Flaco. For some reason I sense with greater awareness the indifference and deafness to the miserable wailing in their hearts. Manu captures the depth of my thoughts when he turns to gaze at them. Curled up in a corner, with downcast eyes, they share among themselves stories the world will never know.

"Excuse me, I'll be right back," I inform. My cellie follows me as if guessing what I'm about to do.

"Hey, homeboys. What's up," I greet the three youngsters.

"Peace be with you," Manu says solemnly. The guys remain motionless, wondering what kind of greeting this might be.

"What's up, Mikey," Elmo finally acknowledges. "How you feeling?"

"It's been hard, bro," I respond.

"Yeah, I feel you."

"How 'bout you guys? Ya'll keepin' it up?"

"Trying to," Smiley replies sluggishly.

A brief silence hangs between us but Manu breaks it up immediately, "Michael and I would like to make you an invitation."

The guys look puzzled.

"Invitation? Go ahead," Smiley indicates.

"Join us," he tells them, "come sit with us."

"What for? What do you guys do exactly?" Vaquero inquires with interest.

"Come and see," Manu states reverently. Then the three of them, leaving everything on the floor, get up and follow us.

We join the rest of the men and my cellie introduces the new members with excitement. The whole group reacts with a joy that permeates, at least for an instant, the wicked atmosphere.

"You're a blessing to the group," Grandpa states with an air of wisdom as the rest concurs by shaking the men's hands. Although there is a tinge of embarrassment in the grimace of the new fellows, Big Bear and Manu, ironically the toughest in appearance, squeeze their shoulders with affection, turning their discomfort into radiant grins.

Eddie leaves the group for a moment, then comes back carrying four small Bibles to distribute among the new guys.

"This is our sword," Eddie proclaims, holding up a Bible, "but the book itself is meaningless if we don't carry its message in our hearts."

"Amen!" the men respond with optimism.

"As you all know," Manu takes over, "we meet around this table every day. But our purpose is not just to keep the Word among us; our goal is to go out and preach the Good News to others, and hopefully not with a Bible in hand, but with our actions. Wherever a good Christian goes, he brings hope, joy, love, compassion, forgiveness. It's time to tear down the walls of indifference and vengeance. We must escape the fences of hatred and begin to turn this hell into a safe environment, full of hope."

Although Manu teaches as one who has authority, some of the new men purse their lips as if deeming Manu's discourse an impossible mission, and yet with a sparkling willingness to do their best. As for me, there are still pangs of nagging doubts in the back of my mind, but I'm determined as well to give it a try.

"I know it sounds crazy," Manu continues as if predicting some of our inner reactions, "but if we do our part, our Father in heaven will do His. So cheer up!"

We all make a circle around the table as Manu sits on its cold surface. Officer Serrano, realizing the group has increased in number, stares apprehensively at us and through the intercom inquires about the meeting. Manu elevates his Bible as if to indicate that the purpose of the congregation is well-intentioned. Serrano grunts his consent.

"Today I wanna talk to you about Forgiveness. I'm sure all of us at some point in our lives have had the desire to forgive or be forgiven. So I wanna start by asking you something: what do you think forgiveness is all about?"

We look at each other a few seconds, then Roger, raising his hand a little, timidly explains, "I read somewhere that forgiveness is like a process in which we seek to get rid of hatred, anger, bitterness and hurt feelings that poison our hearts and minds. And the reason it's called a process is because it's something that doesn't happen overnight. It might take a day, a month, a year, or maybe a lifetime."[10]

Manu nods in agreement. Then Ricky, scratching his chin as if trying to put the words together in his head, breaks in, "I think of forgiveness as some sort of spiritual surgery that we do on ourselves so we can extract the poison that festers our soul because of a hurt or injustice."

"Good," my cellie affirms.

"Forgiveness to me," Thomas adds, "is a gift we give ourselves so that we don't remain stuck in the past and in our pain, living as victims of some painful tragedy." Thomas stops all of a sudden. A stabbing knot in his throat forces him

---

[10] My references to Forgiveness have been influenced by Father Eamon Tobin, author of *How to Forgive Yourself and Others* (Liguori, MO: Liguori, 2006).

to remain quiet for a few seconds. We all wait for him to recover while Eddie pats his shoulder sympathetically. The blistering noise in the block grows louder but it's smothered again as Thomas regains control of himself and begins to read a note he pulled off his Bible with a faltering but loud voice, "Forgiveness is an act of the will; it is the choice we make to let go of the desire to get even. Choosing not to forgive is a decision to continue suffering spiritually, physically, and emotionally. We have to humbly recognize, my brothers, that refusing to forgive keeps us from experiencing real love and genuine peace."

"Very well said," Manu exclaims excitedly, "I am very amazed at the way you perceive and understand forgiveness. You guys made very good points, especially when you mentioned that it has the power to heal us in many ways. I was reading the other day that many psychological studies show that people who learn to forgive tend to have fewer heart problems and diminish the risk to suffer physical traumas, illnesses related to stress, and even depression. Their studies also found that the first step to rehabilitation and transformation of our lives is to recognize the need to forgive those who have hurt us, especially if it's a family member or someone close to us. Roger pointed out that forgiveness is a process, and it's true. It takes time to forgive. There will be times when you'll feel the desire for revenge again, even though you thought you had already forgiven your offender. But true forgiveness is not about forgetting or pretending that an offense never occurred; genuine forgiveness is about remembering the harm done to us and still choosing to forgive."

"Amen!" some of the men echo. Manu turns to Grandpa, and with a slight hand motion offers him an opportunity to share his wisdom with the group.

He agrees.

"Forgiveness restores life," the old fellow begins, looking

intently at all of us.

Someone's shadow approaches me from behind. From the corner of my eyes I make an effort to see who it is but I can't. He then grips my shoulder and motions me to follow him to my cell. I obey without reluctance. Grandpa recognizes him immediately but pretends to overlook the scene and continues his discourse without interruptions. His gaze begs me to be careful.

"Necio came up to me, Michael," Isidro explains as we enter my cave. "He ordered me to kill you."

"What?" I react, with my heart pounding in my ears.

"He said it was either you or me."

"Isidro, do you even know why I don't chill with them anymore?"

"Of course I know. He wanted you to hunt me down. That's why I'm here. Came to set up a plan. Let's get rid of that bastard."

"What? You serious?"

"Come on, *ese*. There ain't no other way."

"I'm sorry, homie, but I can't… I mean…"

"Michael, I don't wanna hurt you. And I know you feel the same way about me. This fool is not gonna leave us alone."

"I gotta think about it, man."

"Well, you better think fast, homeboy, cuz that fool wants you down by tomorrow evening."

"Meet me after dinner at the library."

"Alright. Gotta go. I don't want them bastards to see me getting out of your cell."

Another nightmare has just begun.

"I can't believe this," I whisper, hiding my face in my hands, helpless. I lie on my bed while anguish and hopelessness enter once again through the crack under the door, then voices. The walls seem to distill voices, hundreds of them; secretive voices that seem to be whispering something to me as a pace back and forth, like a buzzing in my ears.

"Stop!" I scream as I leave the cell. I intend to rejoin the group but officer Serrano frustrates my intention by growling my last name, "Moreno, to the door!"

Everyone turns around as if they all had the same last name and briefly scan two individuals dressed in white, waiting in the hallway with a paper block holder. They look like people from the infirmary. One of them toys with a pen as he examines my movements and expressions.

"Hi, Mr. Moreno," the young lady salutes extending her delicate hand, "I'm Dr. Carter, please come with us." The male doctor simply fakes a smile and nods a greeting.

Two guards suddenly appear and escort the three of us to a small holding cell.

"How are you feeling today?" she inquires as she motions me to sit down on a plastic chair, right in front of them. The two officers remain outside with the door open.

Something is not right here. Since when are these people interested in one's wellbeing?

"Who are you?" I respond, dodging her question.

"I introduced myself a minute ago as Dr. Carter. This is Dr. Shawn. We're from the psychiatric department. There's been a concern about you. We just need to evaluate certain things about your..."

"I'm sorry, doctor," I interrupt abruptly in a soft and faintly irritated voice, "I'm doing perfectly fine. I don't need to speak to anybody."

"Mr. Moreno," Dr. Shawn utters, with a slight anger creeping into his words, "we're not suggesting by any means that you're..."

"Crazy?" I break in without even knowing if that was the term he wanted to use, "Of course I'm not. And now, please, I need to get back to my place; I already told you I have nothing to say to you."

The guards poke their heads in, and with a penetrating look ask the doctors if they need their intervention.

"Everything is fine," the woman exclaims, "It's just that Mr. Moreno is not ready to talk about his problem."

"Problem?" I react, raising the tone of my voice, which is lowered again by the officers' threatening eyes. I breathe in deeply, then out, and with this long breath I seem to relax a bit. "If you say I have a problem, then you're probably right: I'm not ready to talk about it. So, please, let me go back to my cell, figure out what my problem is, and then I'll be more than happy to discuss it with you."

The doctors immediately detect the loads of sarcasm in my statement but reluctantly agree with it.

"Okay, Mr. Moreno. We'll definitely come back to see you."

I'm led back to the tank by the two correctional officers. Then I hesitantly approach the religious gathering, with my head hanging. Some turn slightly around to indicate a welcome back.

"Some people hold grudges deep inside," Manu preaches confidently, "even when the offender has for long been dead. That's very unfortunate and unfair for them because they're simply depriving themselves of the joy of living."

"But don't you think some wounds are way too deep to forgive and let go?" Brains asks with an aura of defensiveness but respectful.

"It's true. Some hurts are so deep that many people believe their offender doesn't deserve their forgiveness. But I ask you: do we deserve God's forgiveness and mercy for our many offenses against Him and others? Once again, forgiveness is a process that may take years; and those who refuse to enter the process are simply choosing to give their offender ongoing control over their emotional, spiritual, and physical life. You have the right to believe, my brother, that your offender doesn't deserve your forgiveness, but you shouldn't deprive yourself of the right to be free of all resentment, pain, and all the stress that steals your joy."

"You're right in saying that some hurts are deep, son," Grandpa points out, "but that's precisely when we desperately need God's grace and urgent help. Some hurts may have to be forgiven seventy times seven. Unfortunately, many of us turn away from God during our mourning and sorrow, often blaming Him for our afflictions. But I tell you, if we have a broken relationship with God, we will never be empowered to offer forgiveness."

Brains nods several times, showing that he liked what he heard. Manu gets off the table and thanks the group for their openness and sharing.

We all shake hands and energetically encourage each other. Then we break up. Manu and I return to our cell, but, suddenly, on our way there, a man with a severe anxiety attack appears in front of us.

"I heard you're a good man," he declares trembling, with drops of cold sweat trailing down his forehead.

"Much less, my brother. Only God is truly good," Manu responds compassionately. "What can I do you for you?"

"Could you pray for me?" the troubled man requests.

Manu pulls out a handkerchief and delicately dries off the man's sweat. My jaw drops in amazement as others seem to freeze by his action. After a brief prayer over the shivering man, Manu hugs him tightly and whispers something in his ear. Then he disappears among the crowd.

"Wow, bro," I tell Manu as we enter our cell. "That must've taken some courage."

"Not courage, Mikey. It takes love."

"Well, I would certainly need more than love to do that."

"Michael, what's going on?" My cellie inquires, changing

the conversation abruptly.

"What do you mean?"

"The kid out there, you left the group and followed him here. Is everything alright?"

"No, Manu. Things ain't good," I respond, sitting on the edge of my bunk.

"What happened now?"

"Necio wants revenge."

My cellie leans against the wall, staring at me with a question mark, almost like a prosecutor expecting a detailed account of what happened. I explain to him everything about our rivalry and why Isidro is involved in such a mess.

"So now you're planning to take him down?" Manu reproaches, "Michael, do you have any idea what you're getting into? You mess with one, you mess with the whole gang!"

I remain silent for a while, agitated, knowing he's absolutely right. My cellie paces back and forth, embroiled in a marsh of confusion.

"We need to think of something," he finally declares, "you can't just murder him, that's not a solution."

"Come on, man!" I grunt, feeling a thick wave of baffled rage and anxiety smash within me.

"There must be something we can do without using violence, Michael."

"Oh yeah? Like what?" I scream at him as I get up, "Manu, this is a prison! This is the only way!"

I can't believe I just said that. I feel ashamed.

"No! No!" my cellie begs, seizing my shoulders, "Please, homeboy, wake up! We were not created for this."

Tears well up in his eyes. He wants to speak but chokes on his words.

"I'm sorry, man," I mutter, "I'm just not like you." Then I leave the cell, only to be shocked by a disturbing, unbelievable scene. There, in the far end of the unit, my eyes witness the unimaginable. With an aura of courage and his arms calmly crossed, Grandpa dialogues with Necio.

I stop in my tracks while a million thoughts assail what's left of my ruined mind. Then I sprint back to the cave.

"What's wrong," my cellie inquires, perceiving the rush of adrenaline in my breathing.

"Hey, *ese*. Go watch what Grandpa's doing!"

I wait in the cell and he takes forever to return. I go back out and freeze again. Manu has joined their conversation! An ominous uncertainty sweeps over me, causing a nauseous growling in my stomach. I glance around but none of the religious guys are in sight.

"Damn!" I bark as my feet trudge back to my cage and wait. A few minutes later, Manu enters the cell looking like he just accomplished something; his calmness instantly gives some relief to my anxiety.

"Man, what the hell," I exclaim immediately, "what were you two doing over there?"

"Take it easy, my friend," he advises, reclining on the door, "he's not gonna bother you anymore."

"What? Just like that?"

"Well, I really don't know what Grandpa said to him. When I approached them I simply told Necio that you wanted a change in your life, and he agreed to step back and leave you two alone."

"What?" I respond with growing suspicion, "us two? You mean everything is cool with Isidro as well?"

"Yep, so I'd suggest you tell him there's been a change of plans."

"Wait, how do you know…" I gaze at him, frowning.

"Michael, you've already given yourself the opportunity to see and understand that there's another world beyond the razor wire; that there's more to live and die for. You're walking in the right direction; don't go back to the quicksand. Please. I'm here for you. You can trust me."

I sit down.

"I'm sorry, bro," I utter, clasping my hands, "I'm such a loser."

"Don't say that, Mikey. You're worth more than you can imagine. If you only knew how much God loves you…"

"Please, cellie, not now," I raise my voice a little, then walk up to him and fix my eyes on his. "Thank you for all you do for me, homeboy," I whisper.

I gulp and open my arms to hug him. The walls seem to melt down as my cellie squeezes me warmly for a few seconds, then we exchange a smile and get ready for dinner.

In the chow hall, I'm immediately surrounded by some of the religious group.

"I wanted to thank you for what you did," I declare, gazing at Grandpa who sits across the table, but the disturbing clattering in the background doesn't allow him to hear what I said, so we both lean forward and I repeat my gratitude. "I don't know how you did it, but thank you."

"Not a problem, son. Things will be fine. You'll have the opportunity to focus on school and other things you like."

"That's right, my brother," Eddie adds with his usual exaggerated grin, "and we gonna be there to lend a hand and watch you succeed."

"No doubt about it," Thomas echoes, cautiously licking the whipped cream off his bland little piece of cake.

"I'll certainly do my best, and thank you to you guys as well. I know I'm very stubborn, and you guys have been very patient with me. You've really taught me a lot in just a few days. I never thought I'd meet people like you behind these walls. I've been so blind all this time."

"It's never too late, Mikey," Eddie jumps in, resting a hand on my shoulder, "just try to do your best from now on. And if you fall, it's okay; somebody once said that to get up over and over again after a fall is much more pleasing to God than if we never failed at all."

I smile.

"Try to see each day as if it was your last opportunity to make things right," Thomas adds as he gets up to collect our trays.

The guards patrolling the area frown skeptically at us, then at their surroundings, pacing back and forth like automatons in an almost perfectly straight line. A strident sound, similar to a train whistle, coming from the speaker signals that it's time to cage back in the tank. The officers bark at us to hurry. Then, suddenly, an unkempt inmate pulls my cellie's shirt from behind and joyfully thanks him for a supposed miracle. It's the troubled prisoner Manu prayed over earlier before dinner.

"I feel so much better now," the guy explains, "I don't know how it happened, but I'm sure God listened to your prayer. Thank you, Emmanuel."

"You're welcome, brother. I'm glad you're feeling better."

"Move, move!" the guards howl, breaking the almost mystical encounter with the man.

"Wow, so prayer does work," I tell Manu with a mixture of amazement and teasing.

"You have no idea, my friend. Anyone who has faith in God will do even greater things than this."

When we arrive at the compound, Manu enters the cell as I wander around looking for Isidro, but he's nowhere to be seen. I go to his place to search for him. He opens the door and invites me in. I begin to explain everything but he refuses to believe me, arguing and suggesting that everything is a set-up.

"Just tell me a good reason why you'd believe what he says," Isidro responds infuriated. "You think he's gonna listen to that old man? You saw what they did to him, man!

We gotta do something."

For a moment I'm almost convinced by his anxious attitude, which is nothing other than his adrenaline and desire to survive in this jungle.

"I get your point, bro," I tell him calmly, "but I'm willing to take the risk and trust Mr. Johnson and my cellie. They're good people, Isidro."

"I don't doubt they're good guys, Mikey," he snaps back, raising his voice, "But it's not about them, it's about Necio. I don't trust that bastard."

"I don't trust him either, but I pray he'll keep his word."

"What?" Isidro yells at the top of his voice with spasms of unbelief, "what did you say?"

"I'll pray for all of us. Things will be fine, homeboy."

"Come one, man!"

Isidro sits on the edge of his bunk and hides his face in his tremulous hands. I wrap my arm around his neck and, like a mischievous child, he reclines his head on my shoulder.

"I don't wanna die here, Michael," he confesses between twinges of despair, "I wanna go back to my wife and watch my little baby grow."

"You will, homeboy. You will."

We hug each other goodbye. My cellie waits for me right outside the cell, concentrating on reading a book despite the grumbling of a throng playing cards around a nearby table.

"I'm gonna run a little bit," he tells me, "are you staying here, or you wanna come over with us?"

"Us? Who's us?"

"Eddie invited all the men, but I don't know exactly who's going."

"Sure, why not."

When officer Martinez opens the gate for recreation, everyone hurriedly dashes to the door. Grandpa waits patiently by the entrance, staring at the floor.

"Enjoy, gentlemen," the old fellow expresses, with his face slightly troubled. "I'm not feeling well."

My cellie and I look at each other.

"What's wrong?" I ask.

"My head. I need to go for my check-up. I'll be fine."

"Did they give you any pain killers?" I inquire, noticing his efforts to suppress what seem like unbearable pangs in his head. He clenches his teeth repeatedly.

"What they give you here is always useless. I swallowed a couple of them but still no relief."

"Whatcha waiting for?" Martinez grumbles, "you stayin' or what?"

Grandpa makes his route to the infirmary as Manu and I head outside the building through the long corridor and countless doors slamming one after the other. The rest of our friends gather by the basketball court.

The sky is a bit cloudy. It's that season again when the December wind blows cold, poisoned with the nostalgia of spending Christmas away from home. The gray clouds fuse with the sunset, which is bordered by the brown of some faraway deserted small hills.

As I approach the men, my eyes grow bigger in disbelief. Among them, with his timid smile, is Isidro shaking everyone's hands. I run towards them with a huge grin on my face. Manu does the same.

Isidro greets me with his usual elaborate handshake and a quick hug.

"Our brother here," Eddie indicates, "has joined the brotherhood." His face blushes but Manu squeezes his shoulder gently and invites him to sit with us at the table in the compound. Isidro agrees, asking that we be patient with him. Then after a few laughs and some encouragement, we disperse out into the yard.

I follow Manu around the running track, jogging with

him at his pace. As the heaviness of my sweat increases, the imposing walls and fences seem to grow taller. I stop to drink some water while Manu continues his route. Then my heart beat accelerates when I notice a group of men coming towards me. They still wear their armor of arrogance and grip a shank of hatred but I maintain my composure. It's Necio and three of his men. Their ominous presence automatically makes me clench my fists.

"No, no, no, Mikey," he exclaims mockingly, "don't worry, we're not here to hurt you, right, homeboys?" They all take turns to drink water from the font. "You got a nice daddy in the unit," Necio continues, referring most probably to Grandpa. I want to respond but I force myself to keep quiet. Then I wipe my face off and resume my exercise, leaving the clan behind me. They make no effort to harass me.

I find my cellie further ahead resting on a bench and explain to him my brief encounter with Necio.

"Let's keep praying for him," he offers, "he's just a confused soul, searching desperately for attention and love; for someone who can guide him back home."

As we set out to run another lap, a man moaning loudly passes by, and my cellie seems to be moved by his weeping. He's probably in his late fifties, bald and skinny.

"Mr. Tucker," my cellie screams at the man, with such a voice that he seems to have known him since the beginning of time, "John Tucker, is everything alright? Is there anything we can help you with?"

The man stops and slowly turns around.

"How do you know my name," the prisoner asks between heartbreaking sobs.

"John," Manu pronounces his name again compassionately, "don't worry. You're a man of great faith. Your daughter will live."

Manu's words penetrate into the prisoner's chained soul, stirring up his deepest feelings and causing even more tears. The dark circles under his eyes give the impression he's been suffering for a while.

"My daughter is dying in a hospital, sir," the man exclaims, falling on his knees right in front of Manu.

"I know, John," my cellie responds kindly, wrapping him with a warm embrace, "but she will recover soon. God has listened to your prayers."

The man shows no disbelief in Manu's encouraging words. He thanks him and stands up drying his eyes with his bare hands. Then he goes his way now enveloped in peace.

I gaze at my cellie with admiration, yet with growing suspicion, wondering what kind of prisoner he might be. If what he said to that fellow is true… how did he know?

"Don't be troubled for what you heard me say to that poor man," my cellie tells me as if reading my thoughts, "as I've told you before, you will see greater things than this, Michael; because anything is possible for those who put their trust and faith in God."

I'm left speechless, immersed in my own thoughts about him.

When we go back to the compound, I take a shower, say a few prayers, and then confusedly collapse on my bed.

CHAPTER SEVEN

The next morning, as I wake up, I'm taken aback by something I had already experienced. A floral fragrance invades the tiny cell again. It is more than a fine scent. The aroma seems to sprinkle a certain harmony and peace all over the walls. I close my eyes and inhale deeply. A flood of blurry images begin to pull my emotions in every direction.

"Manu, you up?" I utter hesitantly, running my hands through my hair.

No response.

I crawl out from between the sheets only to find my cellie's bed empty. I look through the window and watch Manu sitting on top of a steel table, surrounded by a huge crowd. I dress and leave the room.

"Woe to the guards and prison officials!" I hear my cellie proclaim as I approach the multitude, "for they inflict further punishments on the prisoners without realizing that one day they will also find themselves face to face with the courts of heaven. Woe to those corrupted attorneys who use the system to illicitly accumulate wealth, for every unjust sentence they imposed on you will be doubled on them in the afterlife. Woe to those gangs that abuse and oppress the vulnerable! for one day, when they grow old and fragile, life shall impose on them greater afflictions."

Elmo, Smiley, and Vaquero, seeing the astonished reaction of the crowd, look at each other with silly grins, as if feeling proud of my cellie.

Some begin to murmur with suspicion, looking every now and then at officer Serrano who appears to be listening intently from the picket.

"Blessed are those crippled by the prison system," Manu proclaims with great authority, "for they shall fly higher than everyone else in heaven. Blessed are those who are imprisoned unjustly, for they shall sit closer to God's throne, accompanied by legions of angels. Blessed are those prisoners forgotten by family and friends, for their names will be written in heaven with the rays of the sun."

Certain prisoners grumble among themselves, "By what authority is this con saying those things? Who is he anyway?"

Serrano becomes uncomfortable with the huge crowd and demands its immediate break-up. Most of the men gathered thank Manu for his encouragement and message, which they understand to be loaded with great hope and challenges.

Immensely delighted, I walk towards my cellie, grip his hand and then give him a tight hug.

"What's that all about?" he tells me surprised.

"I just feel grateful to God that you're here, homeboy."

"And I'm very glad to see that spark in your eyes."

"Hey, ya'll," Elmo exclaims as he comes closer, along with Smiley and Vaquero. They all extend their hands to shake ours.

"That was great," Smiley expresses, referring to Manu's preaching, "I sure believe what you said, brother. And I wanted to ask you something, if you don't mind."

"Go ahead."

"It's about what you shared on forgiveness yesterday. I

was telling the homeboys here that I'm struggling to forgive somebody, but I'm doing the best I can cuz it's really killing me inside, you know. Anyway, the issue is: how do you know when you've forgiven someone?"

"That's a good one," I whisper, identifying myself with his struggle.

"Smiley," my cellie states, placing his hand on the youngster's shoulder, "this is not probably what you wanna hear, but we know that forgiveness is taking place in our hearts when we can pray for our aggressor, wish him well, and let go of all desire to get even. If you're really walking hand in hand with God, He will guide you and give you the strength to forgive the unforgivable."

"By that, you're not suggesting a possible reconciliation, right?" I declare in a sort of defensive way, feeling that his response is too demanding.

"No. With God's grace we can always forgive an offense that a person has committed against us, but we cannot always restore the relationship because the other person may not be interested, or is simply not sorry for his wrongdoing. It only takes one person to forgive, but it takes two to reconcile a hurt."

Although my heart agrees with my cellie's precepts, my mind still struggles to assimilate certain things. Smiley and the others continue their questioning while I excuse myself to go check on Grandpa.

I strike his cell door with an open hand as I peek through the window, with my nose pressed to the glass. I see him lying on his bed, immobile. I open the door slowly, then I poke my head inside.

"Grandpa, can I come in?"

I hear him clear his throat with great effort, then he utters a few words that are difficult to understand. I go in and sit on my haunches, close to his bunk. He barely looks alive. His face is transparent, as if the blood had drained from it, and his hands are all shriveled, nothing but wrinkled claws. His eyes refuse to recognize me.

"Oh, sorry, it's you Michael," he finally stammers, trying to touch my face with his trembling hands. "I can't see very clearly." His voice is weak and muffled, as though he were talking to himself.

"Grandpa, what's wrong with you?" I inquire sadly. "You need to go to the infirmary; you look really bad."

"No, I'm fine," he falters, tossing sideways, "I went yesterday evening, remember? They said I'll be fine. It's just a matter of time. Those pills they gave me only made me feel worse."

"Oh, God," I sigh with remorse. I close my eyes briefly and say a little prayer for him, holding his hand. "You're gonna be fine, Grandpa," I manage to voice as a knot begins to form in my throat.

He squeezes my hand gently.

"I'm gonna get you some soup," I offer as I get on my feet.

"Thank you, son," he mumbles.

I walk back out, directly to Manu and the others, and explain to them in detail Grandpa's physical condition, also asking them to fetch something for him to eat. Vaquero immediately volunteers to provide the instant soup and offers the rest of us a snack. We all nod and thank him for his kindness as we make our way to Grandpa's place.

We find Grandpa coughing and with a severe fever. Manu falls on his knees and uncovers half of his body. Then he takes a clean sock, damps it in the sink, and places it on his forehead.

"Thank you," he utters softly. Manu smiles sadly and begins to pray quietly.

"You're gonna be fine, Mr. Johnson," Smiley whispers. Then Vaquero enters the cell with a small plastic bag full of snacks and hot noodle soup. He tosses the bag on the miniature wooden desk and carefully bends over Grandpa. Manu removes the wet cloth and helps our sick friend sit on the edge of the bunk while Vaquero gingerly places the Styrofoam cup near his chapped lips. Grandpa takes a few sips but chokes, slightly vomiting on his shirt. He apologizes and makes another effort to swallow the hot soup but coughs again.

"Would you like some tea instead, Grandpa?" My cellie offers, cleaning our friend's shirt with some toilet paper.

"Yes, I think that'd be better. Could you get me some?"

"I'll be right back."

I follow my cellie all the way to Isidro's room. Since he works in the kitchen, we figure he might have a few tea bags. We knock on his door several times but get no response.

"He might still be in the kitchen," I suggest.

"Yeah, probably. Let's go ask D.D., he usually trades those things."

D. D. is a huge black male, an alleged leader of a known dangerous clan in the prison. I hesitate to go with Manu but my feet follow him as if they had a mind of their own.

"Hey, brother," my cellie greets him with an aura of confidence, respect, and authority, "I was wondering if you had a few tea bags for trade. Any flavor."

The enormous prisoner scans my cellie with certain respect, but shoots a quick gaze of disdain at me. Then he addresses Emmanuel, "How is it that you, a Mexican, ask a trade of me, a black man?"

"My friend," Manu peacefully states, "it's neither me nor the trade that matters; it's the person who'll drink this tea. If you only knew how happy he'll be because of a single tea bag, you'd be willing to trade the whole box. And yet, it's not the tea he needs; it's the love with which it's given to him."

The muscled man lowers his guard after that response,

and his tough expression seems to have melted into compassion. He motions us to wait as he enters his cell. After a little while he comes back out and hands my cellie a small paper bag.

"Go ahead and take it; you owe me nothin'," the mean gangster utters in a husky tone.

"Heaven is full of people like you," Manu tells him, then shakes his hand. I simply gaze at him gratefully as we head back to Grandpa's room.

"We need some hot water," says Manu, emptying the bag on the desk.

"I'll go get it," Vaquero quickly replies, and when he comes back I offer to prepare the drink myself. I sit next to Grandpa to help him hold up the cup.

When he finishes, the men hold hands and say a little prayer over him. They all hug him gently and take off, promising to come back to check up on him.

"I'm sorry, it's all my fault," I declare, damping the sock again and placing it on his forehead.

"My boy," he murmurs, clearing his throat, "I would do what I did again if necessary. Please, don't blame yourself. It's all part of life. Maybe it's time for me to go. The doctors told me some horrible news yesterday."

"Please, don't say that, Grandpa. You still have a lot to do around here. You're gonna help me with school, remember?"

He giggles slightly and with difficulty; and closing his eyes, a sweet aura of peace takes over the small cell.

"You're gonna go out and be free," I encourage as I squeeze his bare feet softly, "and meet up with your loved ones."

"Michael, I've done some horrible things," he stammers without opening his eyes, "I'm never getting out of here. My mistakes are too many and too big."

"But God is good, remember? God's love and

compassion are greater than any of our sins. You told me that."

"It's true and I believe that. Great are my sins; greater my repentance; and much greater are God's love and forgiveness."

"Then God has already forgiven you; you have a good heart, Grandpa. And you're gonna get up soon, you'll see."

"Thank you for being here, son. I don't want to die alone."

"You're not gonna die, Mr. Johnson. You're gonna be fine."

A strange powerlessness invades my entire being as I watch Grandpa tighten his jaw with all his might, as if trying to suffocate the tremendous pain exploding in his head. His body begins to convulse and I don't know what to do. I run out of the cell, straight to the picket, and explain to officer Serrano what's taking place.

"What's that to you," he responds with indifference, "he ain't related to you, is he?"

"Come on, man," I spit in anger, "it's a human being."

He sneers at me while grabbing the phone.

"Michael," my cellie calls out, "what happened?"

"He's not doing well. I just told Serrano, and he's gonna get the meds."

We go back to Grandpa's place and find him vomiting in the toilet, struggling to hold up his body on his trembling legs.

We put him back in bed, and, surprisingly, in about fifteen minutes, the medical personnel arrive and take our good friend to the infirmary.

Manu and I return to our cell.

"Hey, cellie," I utter, thumbing through the Bible. "I don't mean to be nosy, but, do you know how long Grandpa's sentence is?"

"I don't know. Nobody really knows. Some people say he petitioned to spend the rest of his life in prison."

"What? Why would he do that?"

"I don't know, Mikey. Like I said, that's just what some people say."

A brief silence hangs between us.

I read a few passages from the sacred book and begin pondering about the many things that have occurred lately.

"Cellie," I break the silence, "why is one of the prison commandments about self-pity? 'STOP FEELING SORRY FOR YOURSELF', what exactly does it refer to?"

"It's basically begging you to reconcile with your past and make peace with it so it won't screw up your present and future."

I smile.

"Seriously. It's simply inviting you to take control of your life and remove the label of victim once and for all. If someone caused you pain, yes, you're a victim and have the right to be angry. But you have to make an agreement with yourself and decide for how long. It is not fair for you to suffer for the same event every time you remember it. You cannot allow yourself to be a victim forever.

"It's true that a hurt can have long lasting effects, but ultimately you are in control of your life, of your thoughts and reactions. It will take you time to heal, of course, but you can't allow a painful event to change the entire course of your life. Being angry at life, or at someone forever is a decision to become bitter and miserable. And you don't deserve that."

"Homeboy," I utter while closing the Bible, "I really wanna make the effort to forgive and let go. I want a real change in my life. I'm tired of blaming everyone for all the crap I've been through. I know I've made a lot of mistakes, but I've decided to give myself the opportunity to become a new person. I don't wanna spend the rest of my life behind this razor wire. I know I can do better."

The glow in my cellie's eyes once again tell me I can trust in him. The dim light fuses with the peaceful atmosphere, making the walls around us look like transparent, long curtains, and the floor beneath us like polished marble. I don't know what Manu will do with what I tell him, but I certainly feel the need to pour out everything that has been damaging my world, affecting my relationship with others and my God. I have never spoken to anyone else about this.

"Cellie," I say, almost whispering, "I have to let this out, right now, and I hope you can keep this between you and I."

"My dear homeboy, you know I'm here for you. And I would never, ever, betray your confidence in me. You can tell me anything you want; I promise I will never tell anyone."

He leans on the wall facing my bunk while I let silence take over for a few seconds. I run my fingers through my hair, looking for a way to begin.

"When I was a little boy, maybe six or seven, something happened; something that changed my life completely." I gulp as broken flashbacks begin to run through my head like a distorted old movie.

"My brother Abraham was four and my little sister Alicia was only two. We lived on the Westside of San Antonio. My mom and dad seemed to have a good relationship in the first few years of marriage, but everything changed when my dad had an accident at work that paralyzed his legs. Eventually, through rehab, he started to move his legs again and was able to walk using a cane, but he was never the same. He grew bitter and blamed God and everyone else for his condition. My mom tried to please him in everything, and very slowly she became his slave, one that was never good enough, according to my dad. Then he began to drown his problems in alcohol and became a ruthless monster. The slightest noise in the house bothered him. I wouldn't dare to cry in front of him because I feared I'd get beat up. My mom was a good woman; she always worked hard to pay the rent and feed us all while my dad pretended to babysit us in the afternoons and sometimes late in the evenings.

"One night, my mother came back late from work. She tried to open the front door but it was locked and blocked with a heavy sofa.

"'Open the door, Alejandro!' she desperately shouted my dad's name, but he couldn't hear her because of the loud music and the horrible screams of a next door neighbor, and another drunk-ass who sang along. She hurriedly went around the house and broke through the back door.

"'Michael!' she yelled as she stumbled on the trash can, 'Abraham!'

"She inspected the kitchen and tensely searched the living room but didn't find anyone. The screams and the deafening music came from my parents' bedroom. She forced the door open and was stunned by the horrible scene she witnessed: my father danced, half naked, holding my little brother Abraham in his arms as the other two men clapped and cheered to the rhythm of the music.

"My mother became breathless and was overcome by wrath. She wanted to scream but she couldn't. Nobody noticed her standing at the door. Filled with unbridled rage, she lunged towards the drunk dancers, pushing the fat one aside and snatching my little brother from my dad's arms. He immediately became furious, smashed his beer can on the floor and seized her by her long hair. His violent action made her drop Abraham on the ground, hitting his head.

"Then my father slapped her in the face, forcing her to pick up his beer. She screamed in terror. The two men got scared and backed away when my father, lame as he was, kicked my mother's head, making her whole body convulse.

"My dad turned the music off as my little brother's heartbreaking weeping echoed through the nasty room. Realizing that my mother's body wasn't moving, the three men finally staggered out abandoning the place.

"A little later, my mom recovered from her trauma. She painfully managed to sit on her knees and then crawl slowly towards my brother who cried inconsolably. She hugged him tenderly and covered his face with kisses. In her distraught pain and misery, my mother hadn't noticed my little sister's cold body lay near the bed, stained with blood. She screamed in despair."

The guard's voice through the intercom interrupts my account with the announcement that maintenance personnel is urgently needed on the second floor. Manu is looking at me so intently that he almost appears to have been hypnotized. My voice breaks a little before continuing.

"My father had dropped my little sister on his way out to the corner store, hitting her head unconscious on the concrete steps. He had put her down on a small couch, covering her body. He was already drunk and falling asleep with a beer in his hand when the other two men showed up at the house, both drunk. The front door was open so they entered without permission. I hid in my room with my little brother. The fat man knocked on my door twice and then pushed it open when he got no response. I hugged my little brother in fear.

"'Where's daddy?' he asked, mocking a little kid's voice.

"'In his room,' I stuttered. The bald one came closer and took my brother with him, leaving me alone with the other man. He locked the door and sat on the edge of my bed, looking at me with lust.

"'I'm not gonna hurt you, kid,' he whispered. I grabbed a pillow and hugged it tightly, trembling. He caressed my hair, sliding his rough hand down my face. With a perverse smile on his reddish face, he began to hum a children's song and then snatched the pillow I held in my arms and flung it to the floor.

"I was an innocent child. I didn't know what he was about to do. He took my clothes off, one by one, until he left me totally naked. I was shaking anxiously, looking at him with disgust and sobbing. He took his shirt off, pulled his pants down, and then made me turn around. It was very painful. I screamed and wept in horror but it was useless, the deafening sound of the music playing disguised my cry for help.

"Then I suddenly felt something unexplainable. My soul seemed to abandon my innocent body, as if to keep me from feeling any more pain. I watched the filthy, fat man do to my body all sorts of things. I was lost in anguish; lost in a cruel nightmare. Finally, my tormenter left me to join the others in the front room. That's when my mother came home."

Manu has tears burning his cheeks. His tender look communicates more than compassion; it expresses something I haven't felt in years.

"I'm so sorry, Michael," he stammers as he comes close to me. I get up and we hug each other as hard as we can. His embrace ignites the flame of love deep inside me that had been extinguished for so long. It is a brotherly hug, a compassionate touch that begins to melt down the steel bars in which my heart and my soul have been imprisoned for years. I break down, unable to contain my heavy tears and moans that come from the depths of my being. I close my eyes tightly and it feels like a warm breeze sweeping over us. I don't know why but I can't let go of my cellie's embrace. I feel the burden of sorrow being transformed by a peaceful, luminous aura. Then my tears become heavier as I sense a beautiful scent entering through the porous walls and filling the entire place. I inhale deeply, still embracing while he caresses my head. When we finally let go of each other, he grabs my cheeks with both hands and wipes off the stream of tears still drowning my eyes.

"My dear friend," Manu mumbles in a broken quavering

voice, "I'm so sorry."

We sit on the edge of the bed while a comforting silence descends over us.

"That night, my mom called the police," I go on more calmly, wanting to finish the whole story, "and I never saw my father again. I never told anybody about what happened to me either. I wanted to forget. I wanted to pretend that it never happened, but that horrible experience grew up with me, transforming my innocence into a powerful hatred towards my father and that man."

I pause a few seconds to collect my thoughts and memories.

"We moved away from that neighborhood after that incident hoping to start a new life, and we did. Everything went well for a number of years, until my brother and I started hanging out with the wrong crowd. We both got into the dope business in the hood, and everything turned into hell. I can't speak for my brother, but I was very cruel to my mother. I never appreciated anything she did."

"Where is she now?"

I pause again as a lump suddenly forms in my throat.

"My mom was killed in a robbery," I explain, "She was getting gas near the house, when two masked men ran into the store; and as they were leaving, a police car was pulling in. In that encounter, the robbers, in their anxiety, pulled out their guns, and shot a few bullets at the cops. Unfortunately, a stray bullet hit my mother in the chest."

"Damn, homeboy," Manu expresses, absorbed in the depth of my own feelings.

"It was hard, bro. It was very painful for both of us. My brother couldn't take it. He was also in prison when that happened, and…"

I pause to clear my throat. Manu takes my hand and squeezes it gently, giving me the strength to finish, "he committed suicide."

My cellie shakes his head sadly, then places his arm around me to help me stand. We embrace each other again as true brothers, feeling each other's love and spiritual warmth.

"You guys in there?" we hear someone shout, then several hard smacks on our door. It's Eddie.

"Hey, my brothers," he exclaims as soon as I open the door, "don't mean to bother you, but, is it true what I just heard about Grandpa?"

"Yeah, homeboy," I explain, "he was feeling really bad."

"Dang, man. I hope everythin' turns out good."

"I know, bro. I hope so, too."

"We should get together this afternoon, after lunch, to pray for him."

"That's a good idea. What you think, cellie?"

Manu agrees and congregates the eleven of us right before recreation. Although I make a great effort to listen carefully to their reflection, my mind begins to meander in other directions, closer to home. I can feel my spirit yearning for an encounter with my wife and daughter. When will I see them again, Lord?

"Hey, Michael," someone shouts, but all I hear is echoes, "are you alright?"

I try to identify the voice but I can't. My eyes keep staring at the unit's windows while my ears listen to the hollow footsteps of the guards echoing against the walls.

My brain tells me I must have slept because when I come back to reality my head is tilted and the ends of my lips with spittle.

"Michael?"

"I'm fine, I'm fine," I finally respond, shaking my head.

"Are you sure?" Tony asks, "looks like you got lost, buddy."

"Just a little distracted and tired, that's all."

Manu winks and smiles at me, then motions me to wipe

off the saliva dripping from my chin. They all grin as they resume their sharing.

A little later, officer Martinez opens the gate for recreation, and everyone rushes out to the courtyard like deer fleeing a dangerous forest.

My cellie joins a bunch of men exercising by the baseball area, and I begin to warm up, this time determined to run an extra lap. I run one, two, three laps, then Brains catches up with me, breathing heavily and sweating in his thin shirt like some professional athlete. We greet each other with a smile, and then I suddenly stop when I see someone I know standing where the track curves. Brains does the same, questioned by the look in my eyes flaring wide with anxiety. It's T.J. and three of his men blocking the way. They come towards us, their glowering expression increasing as they get closer.

"Hey, Mikey," T.J. exclaims brazenly, flaunting superiority, "you still owe me a little something. I hope you remember, *ese*."

I stiffen at his words and turn to Brains to signal him to leave.

"I know what I owe you, man," I reply with confidence and even a spark of toughness, "I'll make arrangements next week so you can get your money as soon as possible."

"Mikey. Mikey," he sneers, fidgeting with a dried leaf while his jaw tightens, "don't play with me, fool. It's been three weeks already. You know I got people all over the place watching every move you make; and if you don't play by my rules, you're dead."

I break out in a cold sweat and feel like a vulnerable worm as a wave of feelings battle within me, but I refuse to respond to his threat with violence.

"Look, man," I speak, carefully choosing my words, "I promise you're gonna get your money. It's just a matter of…"

"Is everything aright?" Big Bear interrupts as he

approaches from behind me, accompanied by Manu. Their commanding presence seems to challenge T.J. and his crew, and their intimidating stance immediately turns into anger.

"This ain't none of your business, B.B. Just came to deliver a friendly reminder to our buddy Mikey."

"I know about his debt with you, brother," Manu speaks with calmness and authority, "you'll have your money by Monday."

"You have no idea how much he owes me, Mr. Charity," T.J. huffs angrily while the other puppets adopt a clumsy fighting position, squeezing their fists. The guards on the towers seem to be aware of our growing conflict and shoot a few bullets in the air, scaring everyone else but us.

"Don't worry, you'll have enough in your account," my cellie snaps, then motions us to walk away. The members of the gang are left with their fury, seething through their teeth.

"Quite a few enemies around here, huh?" Big Bear teases. I shrug and apologize for the ugly scene.

We all go back to the compound, and I walk straight to my cave, buried in my thoughts, trying to disentangle a cobweb of ruthless emotions attacking my entire being. I can't rot away in here. God, please help me.

Manu comes in.

"Hey, homeboy, you alright?" he asks, sensing immediately the burden that is making my head sink between my shoulders.

"Yeah, I'm fine," I lie, "I just need to relax." I slouch on my bunk and grab something to read. "Hey, is Grandpa back yet?"

"No, not yet," he responds, "he might be over there all night."

Silence takes over. I cover my head with a pillow as my mind turns into a maze of mixed up thoughts, then, without meaning to, I fall asleep.

CHAPTER EIGHT

The following morning, I get up early for a little workout, and then straight to the showers. Next week, on Sunday, will be Christmas day and I haven't heard anything from my wife and baby girl in months. I begin to bawl openly, like a little kid. Tears of repentance run down my cheeks, mingling with the pouring water of the shower. I wish with all my heart I could see them and tell them about my wanting to change, and that this time I'm serious and stubbornly determined to make plans in which God and family will be top priority.

I finish my shower and hurry back to my cell still bathed in tears. Manu is up, leafing through his book.

"Such an early bird," he comments, smiling.

"Yeah, homeboy, today is Sunday, visitation day for me. I still hope someone will show up."

"I like the 'hope' part," he sighs. "One day, homeboy, there'll be joy, happiness, and peace in your life."

"And when will that be, bro?" I draw a frown smile.

"I don't know; you tell me."

"Manu, I already promised myself I'm gonna do things better; I'm gonna make a positive plan of the things I wanna accomplish next year. I swear I'll stop wasting my time around here and take advantage of the few opportunities available. I know I can do it, it's just that, man, this place makes you go crazy."

"I know you have a great desire to change, Mikey. Keep it up, and don't let go of God's hand. If you keep your promises, God will keep His. Don't let the prison drama kill your good intentions and dreams."

"I won't, homie."

Sitting in front of the tiny desk with a pen and paper, I sigh heavily and stare blankly at the wall for a time, twiddling my thumbs while trying hard to collect my thoughts. I want my words to be exact and profound, honest and with much love. I need to explain to my wife in full detail my latest experiences in this place, especially those that have opened my eyes spiritually, allowing me to dream again and to imagine a beautiful life beyond these walls, together as a family.

As I begin to write the letter, a huge lighting storm of memories strikes at the depths of my mind, making me fall apart and cry silently. The tears collecting around the bottom of my chin fall on the paper, as if my heart and soul desire to write part of the letter.

When I finish, I read it over, fold it, and put it in an envelope. My cellie jumps down from his bed and kindly offers me several snacks for breakfast. He grips his towel and heads to the showers while I sit down to devour a bag of chocolate cookies.

I go out to the common area to get some cleaning supplies from officer Serrano so I can do a little scrubbing in the cell, but the presence of a few people dressed in white watching me from the unit's entrance makes me stop in my tracks. I think it's the same people from the psychiatric department I met with days ago. I frown at them, then switch my gaze towards the guard.

Serrano immediately denies my request, arguing he's running out of supplies. As I beg once again for the items,

Chaplain Lopez shows up with a bunch of books.

"Hey, chaplain, how you doin' today?" the officer asks with a phony tone, "More Bibles! Wow! You really hope these beasts are gonna change some day, don't you?" he so insolently exclaims.

"I certainly do, Mr. Serrano," the chaplain responds softly, acknowledging my presence with a nod and a quick smile, "hope is the only thing I would never allow myself to lose. Believe it or not, I see the very face of God in these men."

Serrano laughs with disdain. "Come on, chaplain. What good can come out of prison? Look at 'em."

"Many people, officer, have fallen into the trap of believing that God could not possibly dwell in each one of us. But we must understand that even with our countless mistakes our good God still calls us to be one with Him."

"Listen, chaplain, these ain't angels behind bars; these are murderers, thieves, and rapists. You'll never convince me to treat them otherwise. But, anyway, who do you wanna see?"

"May I speak with Mr. Eddie Walker, please?" Father Lopez firmly inquires, and the guard grants his request using the intercom.

Eddie comes out to receive the sacred books as I begin to return to my cave. He holds a brief conversation with the chaplain and takes the Bibles to his cell, then he comes back out with some fruits and a noodle soup.

"I'm gonna assume you haven't had your breakfast yet," he tells me, handing me the soup.

We both sit down.

"Well, I had a few cookies just a little while ago but thanks."

"You still need the cleaning stuff?" he asks, biting on his apple with great delight, "Serrano told me you needed some."

"Yeah, you got any?"

"Plenty for both, brother."

"Thanks, man."

"By the way, Michael, I really wanted to say this: there's something different about you."

I chuckle.

"Different? What do you mean?"

"I don't know. There's something in your eyes I couldn't see before."

I secretly agree with him. Even though I cannot fully express what is occurring within me, I'm glad that at least my eyes are able to partially display some of my deepest feelings.

Manu steps out of the restroom area and walks towards us with his towel hanging around his neck. He's about to take a seat when suddenly Serrano, with a grating voice, shouts his last name through the speaker. Two officers wait for him at the entrance.

My cellie shrugs, tossing his towel on the bench, intrigued by the unexpected visit. Then he disappears with them with his hands cuffed.

Thomas approaches the table, with his hair neatly brushed and his face thoroughly shaved, as if expecting a visit. "What's up with Manu?" he immediately inquires, "why they take him?"

"We don't know," I respond, emphasizing with a shrug, "you know these people just come and take you wherever they want."

"I know."

"So how about you, brother," Eddie asks, "you got a visit or what?"

"Well, my wife must be on her way right now," Thomas exclaims with excitement.

"Must be nice, bro," I comment, "how often does she come?"

"Only once a month; the trip is long and expensive, you know."

Thomas' words repeat themselves over and over again in

my mind as if there was a huge echo in the tank: 'the trip is long and expensive.'

"Maybe that's the reason why my wife hasn't come to see me for the past six months," I tell them.

"Money is certainly an obstacle, brother," Eddie says, with an effort to perk up my spirits, "but it's only the tip of the iceberg. You know very well that when a person is incarcerated, the whole family suffers with him. Sadly, we drag our loved ones into this pit, and sometimes we don't even realize the emotional difficulties they have to go through as they cope with the situation. You must understand it hasn't been easy for her either."

"That's right, bro," Thomas adds, "I used to be an asshole with my wife every time I wrote her, but one day I came to understand that if we don't support each other, our relationship sooner or later will turn into dust. Michael, we must accept our reality and assume responsibility for the mistakes we've made, instead of demanding things our wives cannot afford and casting the blame on them. "

I feel a dagger as cold as marble penetrating my chest. Their words are blunt, yet they speak the truth in its fullness. I remember a time when I wrote a letter to my wife, making her feel guilty of all the atrocities that devastated our relationship, and disrespectfully demanding deposits of large amounts of money into my prison account.

"You're right, homeboys," I utter regretfully, "I did all that to my wife and even worse things."

The screeching of the sliding door makes us turn our heads around. There, right at the entrance, a medical staff member and a disheveled officer carelessly escort our good friend Grandpa into the unit. They have removed the bandage from his head but a few small patches still remain. We hurry to the door and embrace him softly, caressing his shoulder and back with affection.

"Come on, kids, it's only been a day," he stammers, with

a huge grin plastered across his face. "I'm joking, my boys, I missed all of you as well."

"How you feelin', Grandpa?" Eddie queries, "Did they tell you anything, any diagnosis?"

"Well, I'm feeling just a little better. They were able to fight off the fever, but my head still feels the size of a mountain. As far as a diagnosis..." And he gulps slowly and intensely, gazing at all of us with such sadness that one would immediately think he has only a few days left to live.

"Don't worry, Grandpa," I utter softly, holding his arm as we make our way to his place, "whatever it is, we're gonna take good care of you. I promise."

"Thanks, my boy."

"Please excuse me, brothers," Thomas tells us, "I'm gonna get ready for when my wife comes."

"Alright," Grandpa says, "be nice to her."

We giggle.

"I'm gonna sleep for a while," Mr. Johnson says as he slowly drops his body on his bunk, gripping my shoulder.

"We'll be checking up on you, Grandpa, just in case you need anything," Eddie and I offer. Then we half cover his body and leave the cell.

"You want the cleaning stuff right now?" Eddie asks.

"Yeah, that'd be good."

"I'll bring it to your room."

"Cool. Thanks, bro."

"Not a problem."

Eddie does come to my cell bringing the cleaning supplies and even helps me with the drudgery of cleaning the place. Then he goes off to meet with some of the brothers at the table as I get ready to do my laundry before the 4 p.m. count. It takes me hours to wash just a few clothing items, but when I'm through I make my way to Grandpa's cave. I enter without asking permission. He's awake and moaning in pain, squeezing his head harshly with both hands.

"Hey, what's wrong?" I exclaim.

"I'm fine, son," he mumbles, "Don't worry, this pain comes and goes. I was feeling a little better a while ago."

"Damn it," I grunt, feeling totally helpless. I sit on my haunches to hold his hand.

"It's alright, son, I can take it."

"I hate to see you like this, Grandpa."

"Don't worry, my boy; I'm fine with it. Remember that suffering is also part of being human. No one can escape it."

"Yeah, I know, but some people just don't deserve it. Why is this happening to you? You're a good man."

"Michael, you don't know me," he gasps, coughing, and dribbling a little, "And in the first place, who are you to judge whether someone deserves pain or not? Suffering, like many experiences in life, lends itself to interpretation. For me the pains of life are no longer a punishment. Instead of crying out to God to be delivered from my suffering, I prefer to rest in Him throughout the pain."

"Well, I'm afraid I'll disagree with you on this one," I mutter softly, "Life has hurt me a lot and the wounds are still deep. I've tried hard to understand why, why me."

"Suffering is not something to be understood, son; it's not something to be questioned; suffering is something to be embraced."

"Come on, Grandpa," I protest, hiding my irritation as I slowly release his hand, "you have absolutely no idea what I've been through; I can't forgive, I can't forget, I can't get on with my life because of a festering wound in my heart. It's an unbearable grudge that's been eating me alive."

"I have told you before that it is in the moments of darkness and pain that God is closest to us. It's in our darkest experiences that we have the opportunity to meet God face to face. Listen to me, son, if there's no suffering, there is no resurrection, no transformation in our lives. Without suffering, without tears, without death, my life would be in a worse condition. It has been through my wounds that God has been able to draw out the best in me. Wounded I remain calm and learn to weep. Weeping, I learn to understand others. God punishes no one, my boy, and now that I've come to know Him a little better, I'm ashamed of the times when I immaturely thought of pain as God's punishment."[11]

His words begin to raise my adrenaline and my skepticism. If he only knew the depths and origins of my resentment, he wouldn't be talking to me in the same way!

I breathe a little heavily, trying to allow his words to sink deeper in my mind and heart.

"You said our pain is not something to be questioned," I complain, "are you implying that suffering is one of those mysteries in life?"

"It's not my intention to state a universal mystery, I only speak from experience. I'm way older than you, son, and, believe me, I stopped a long time ago trying to find explanations for the misfortunes in my life, because I realized that understanding why people suffer doesn't make you a better believer. I discovered that the real question we should all pose ourselves is: What are we doing to help alleviate the suffering in other people's lives? Rather than saying 'why this?', we should focus on 'what can we do about it?'

"But if you want to spend the rest of your life trying to solve the enigma, go ahead. Do it. In the end you will realize that it wasn't worth your time."

"Damn it," I whisper while reclining on the wall with my arms crossed. "Well, I'll certainly give it some thought, Grandpa. I have to admit you're right in a way."

"My boy, please don't wait to be as old as I am to embrace God's gifts for all of humanity. Accept his love, grace, and most especially his forgiveness. Unless you truly accept his forgiveness and infinite mercy, you will never be

---

[11] I like and share Carlo Carreto's understanding of suffering in his book *Why, O Lord? The Inner Meaning of Suffering* (Maryknoll, N. Y.: Orbis, 1986).

able to forgive yourself and those who hurt you."

Seeing that the old man is struggling to communicate what feels like his last testament, a strange sorrow falls over me; and it hurts.

"Thank you for your kind words, Grandpa. You know I'm doing the best I can. Please, be strong; God's on your side."

"Thank you for bearing with me, son."

"Don't thank me, Grandpa; it's the least I can do for you."

As I get ready to leave, Grandpa's cellie excitedly enters the room, the result of a joyful visit with his family. We greet each other quickly on my way out.

Isidro approaches me from behind before I enter my cell. He seems a little worried.

"Yo, bro. I got some bad news," he tells me, unable to conceal his anxiety.

"What happened?"

"You know where they took Manu?"

"I don't know, bro. Do you?"

"Ya, they took him to the hole."

"What?" I exclaim, my voice rising in volume and pitch, "why, what'd he do?"

"I don't know, I asked Martinez but he won't tell me. He said it ain't none of my business."

"Damn it!"

We head to the picket with the intention to beg the officer to tell us the reason behind Manu's captivity, but Necio and some of his pawns appear in front of us.

"Hey, uh, what happened to your friend?" Necio inquires with a mocking attitude, "I heard he's gonna spend some time in a private place."

"That ain't true," I state firmly, "he's in the visitation area."

"Is that so? I thought visits were just two hours long. Man, I wonder why they took such a righteous man to that ugly room." His mockery increases as my blood begins to boil, causing my skin to flush. Isidro grips my arm and takes me away from these fools.

"Watch out, Mikey, they might come for you, too," they burst in laughter.

We ask Martinez about Emmanuel's disappearance, but he refuses to give any explanation. Then Serrano arrives to replace Martinez but we get the same reaction.

"Something tells me Necio's behind all this," I tell Isidro while we walk to Eddie's cell.

"I wouldn't doubt it."

When Eddie opens the door we immediately explain to him what is happening. Then he offers to summon the eleven of us after the count to pray for our friend Manu. I go back to my cell to wait for lunch, and when the trustees show up with the brown paper bags, I take mine and grab an additional one for Grandpa. To my surprise, I find him up and reading a book, pacing slowly back and forth.

"Hey, how you feeling?"

"I feel a little better, son. It's strange how this pain suddenly vanishes."

"Glad you're up, I brought you the usual."

"No kidding."

I place both bags on the little desk. Grandpa takes out something that is supposed to be a sandwich and examines it with his eyes and nose, then he puts it back in the bag, grabbing an apple instead.

"Grandpa," I speak softly, "I think they sent Manu to the hole."

"What'd you say?"

"Two guards came for him this morning but we don't know exactly why. Isidro heard the rumor that he was taken to the hole, and then this fool, Necio, came at us and barked the same thing, that Manu had been locked up in there."

"My God, what could've happened?"

"I don't know, Grandpa, but I can almost assure you that fool had something to do with it."

"Who? Necio?"

"Yeah, he and his men."

"And what makes you think that?"

"By the way he spoke and laughed at us."

"Well, son, as in most situations around here, all we can do is wait and hope for the best."

"I know. Eddie wants us to meet after the count to pray for him."

"Sounds good to me."

I'm starting to believe that hope is really something that should never die within us. It's evident that for these men, prayer, a profound conversation with God, increases their optimism and the belief that something good can always come out of any situation, as hopeless as it may seem. I will certainly pray for my friend Manu; I have been in the hole on quite a few occasions and a single day in there is very close to my idea of hell.

I hug Grandpa goodbye and go back to my cell to take a nap. After a while, Serrano announces that count time has begun. I get up and stand staunchly next to my bunk. When they finish, the doors are unlatched and everyone invades the common area once again. Our group gathers around Grandpa who leads us in prayer, then we begin to discuss the possible reasons that might have gotten our friend Manu in trouble.

"If he's been accused of something," Eddie states, "I totally believe in his innocence."

"I don't wanna point fingers at anybody," I declare, "but I still think Necio has something to do with this."

"Well," Grandpa speaks with a gentle tone, "it's better if we wait. All of our suspicions and speculations are pointless.

We must be patient and wait for tomorrow. Manu is a man of faith and can take care of himself."

We break up and I take Grandpa to his room. Then I return to my cell, grab the letter I wrote earlier to my wife and place it in the outgoing mail tray. I sit down to watch TV for a little while, but seeing that tension begins to build up around the area, I get up and walk straight to my cell, begging the Lord for Monday to hurry.

CHAPTER NINE

I really don't want to wake up.

I know. I was full of hope just yesterday, but that's how it is here; nothing lasts more than a day. Each sunrise finds us in our lonely cells, and with each sunset we slowly die into the night; everything dies. Today is no different; it's one of those days you just want to stay in bed, immobile, immersed in an endless dream.

I get up to use the toilet, then go back to bed.

Suddenly, a military sounding angry voice calls out my last name through the intercom, "Mr. Moreno, get your ass up, someone's here to see you."

I hurriedly get off my bunk, hoping to hear some good news, and peek through the window, but I don't see anything unusual; it's the same ominous environment. I get dressed and head to the picket. Two guards already wait there, impatiently.

"Good morning," I greet in a serious tone. The officers, without responding, grab my shoulders and cruelly put my hands on my back to chain them. I follow them to a private cell.

"Sit down," one of them barks as the other crosses his arms, stabbing me with his eyes.

"Tell me about the escape," he demands furiously.

"Escape?" I mutter, raising my eyebrows.

"Listen to me, con; you don't play with me. I know everything about your plan. Who's the brains behind it?"

"I don't know what you're talking about, man," I huff angrily.

"Better start talking," snaps the other guard, squeezing my neck from behind, "or you're gonna spend a few weeks in the hole."

"Come on, man, I swear I have no idea what you're talking about."

A million thoughts run through my confused mind. Where did they get such an absurd accusation? They stare at me for a while but I remain silent. There is nothing to explain.

"We're gonna give you a chance to think it over. We'll be back."

The officers leave, locking me inside, without removing the shackles binding my hands. I look around. The thick walls and low ceiling seem to squash me. I bow my head and begin to pray.

A few hours later they come back, bringing another member of their hierarchy, a lieutenant. The guards remain standing by the door as their boss arrogantly approaches me and drops his weight in front of me. He's a tall, square-shouldered man wearing a dark brown uniform. He purses his lips and looks directly at me, confidently, yet at the same time he seems to be taken aback, as if he were afraid of me.

"I'm Lieutenant Ibarra," he states, with an edge of toughness in his voice. "Do you know why I'm here?"

"No, sir," I reply, rolling my eyes, with my face cast down, refusing to make eye contact, "please tell me."

He immediately senses a trace of sarcasm in my voice. He clutches his hands and clenches his teeth but makes an effort to speak with calmness, "You know full well, Mr. Moreno, we have very good methods of persuasion here, so please consider telling the truth."

"I've already told your men I know nothing about the so-called escape. How do you even know that a plan is taking place in my unit?"

"I must admit that so far we have no physical evidence of anything, but I swear we're gonna find it. You're not going anywhere, Mr. Moreno. People like you deserve to rot in the darkness of this place."

His last words pierce my soul. I raise my head to look him in the eyes. An unbridled contempt flowing through his pupils extinguishes the glimmer of hope in my own eyes.

"I've been killed a thousand times, Lieutenant," I respond with tears forming in my eyes, "nothing you do to my body at this point will increase my suffering."

"Oh, look," he tells his men mockingly, "the little girl is about to cry."

The guards burst out laughing.

"People like you never change, Mr. Moreno," Lieutenant Ibarra continues, "I've seen many of you come and go, over and over again. If it was up to me, I'd never let anyone leave this place."

I remain silent, making an effort to suppress my tears. Why do I feel hurt by his words?

"How can you expect people to change," I finally challenge, adopting a more calmed composure, "when your system is only dedicated to warehousing prisoners, focusing on harsh punishments and extreme alienation from society? How can you expect us to lead better lives behind these walls when your administration fails to provide rehabilitative programs in which we can actually feel like human beings? Your system, Lieutenant, fails terribly in achieving the real goals of incarceration."

He breathes heavily, like a mad bull, ready to attack. He turns to his men and orders them to take me back to my unit before he vents his fury on me. The officers immediately obey.

Back in the compound, Isidro waits impatiently by my cave.

"Damn, homeboy," he states, "I thought they had moved you."

"No. Everything is fine, homie. They just needed to ask me some questions. Nothing to worry about."

"Glad to hear that, man."

"It was him," I utter when I glance at Necio standing by the restroom.

"Whatcha talking about?"

"Let's go inside."

Isidro sits on the floor while I collapse on my bunk.

"These fools, the guards, are accusing me of trying to break out of prison. They told me about an escape plan. But I don't know anything about it. They think I'm the one mapping everything out. But something tells me Necio is behind all this."

"Necio? How can you be so sure?"

"Think about it. Remember what he said yesterday after they took Manu? He said to watch out, that they might come for us, too. What if he made something up just to mess with these righteous men? What if they took Manu for the same reason, thinking he's the brains behind it?"

"I don't know, man, it all sounds kinda crazy. Necio is everything but a snitch."

"If he had the guts to beat up an old man, I'm sure he wouldn't hesitate to do something like that. Damn, I just hope Manu is okay wherever he is."

"Don't worry bro, Manu has a special something, as if he were protected by God himself."

"It's funny you say that. I was thinking the same thing."

"By the way, I was talking to grandpa and the other guys and they mentioned something about organizing a special gathering for Christmas. What do you think?"

"Sounds great," I respond with enthusiasm, "and hopefully by that time Manu's already back."

"Yeah, I hope so."

We hear someone whistle outside my cell.

It's Eddie. Isidro opens the door.

"It's almost time for lunch, brothers," he tells us as we shake hands, "you guys going?"

Isidro turns to me, and, with a gentle look, convinces me to explain to our friend my earlier experience with the guards. So I begin relating what took place hours before.

"Our friendship is being tested," Eddie reflects, "we must stand firm and stay together. We cannot allow people's lies to destroy our friendship, our community. God is on the side of the just and will never forsake us."

"It's all my fault," I say in a soft and faintly bitter voice.

"No, homeboy," Isidro intervenes, "it's all part of life, part of the test, like Eddie said. And I agree with him: we must be strong and look out for each other."

After lunch, I meet up with Grandpa in his cell.

"Instead of wasting your energies worrying about things that haven't taken place yet," he advises, "you should focus on this."

He shows me several books which he lays on the small desk. "These were part of some courses I had to take for my BA, quite a few years ago. We can start with them."

"I don't get it," I respond, frowning.

"If you're admitted into the University," he explains holding a book, "there are some basic classes you will have to take prior to the core courses of your career. If you begin with these books, which cover the basics, when you're actually enrolled it'll be easier for you."

"So you want me to study as of right now?"

"Yes, my boy. It's important to keep your mind and body

occupied for some time. And like I said before, I'll be by your side helping you."

"I think I like the idea."

"We'll start with three subjects: Biology, Math, and Literature. Read the first two chapters of each book and we'll discuss them tomorrow morning."

He places the three fat books in my hands and kindly pinches my cheeks.

"You'll do well, son. It'll help you stay away from the prison drama."

"I hope so, Grandpa," I sigh.

"I don't hear much enthusiasm in your voice about school now."

"It's not that, Grandpa. I never thought I'd say this, but I miss my homeboy Manu."

"I see. I feel you, son. But I can assure you, he will be back sooner than you think."

"What if he was transferred?"

"Let's hope that's not the case. Come on, show some faith."

I look at Grandpa and cannot help feeling a certain tenderness for him. He looks weak and thinner. The glimmer in his eyes seems to be dying. I wish I knew how to help him. I now understand with much more clarity what he said to me days ago, that one can discover the hiddenness of God in the people around us.

I hug the old fellow goodbye, and back in the cell, I toss into bed and begin reading the chapters as he suggested, highlighting terms and concepts that are unclear to me. I even skip dinner because of my interest in and concentration on the subjects. I manage to finish the readings by midnight. Then after a few prayers, I cover my head and fall asleep.

Early in the morning, after a brief spiritual reflection with the guys, Grandpa asks me to bring the textbooks so he can begin his promised tutoring.

"So which subject are you more comfortable with?" he inquires, eager to share his knowledge. I hadn't realized that he has a few scars on his wrists since he no longer wears the usual white long-sleeve shirt under his khaki clothes. The small patches on his head have been removed, leaving several gashes still covered with tiny particles of dried blood.

"I'm glad your wound is healing quickly," I utter, touching his head.

"Yes, I thank God I'm feeling just a little better today. But don't avoid my question, son."

I smile.

"I think I'm more into this," I respond, opening the Geometry book. "It kinda helps me fly away from this reality for a bit. I've always liked numbers."

"Good, that's the point, to keep your mind busy…"

Grandpa and I spend hour after hour discussing terms, mathematical equations, famous English authors, and many other concepts. His wisdom is enviable. He encourages me to read ahead a few more chapters and be ready to 'teach him' what I learned at our next session. His knowledge and yet great humility with regards to academics is incredible; one could say he's a living encyclopedia; no, possibly an entire library.

I return to my cell and open my books again, eager to know more. Then Ricky and Roger knock on my door, concerned about my self-isolation.

"It's not that I wanna be all alone, brothers," I explain, "I just can't concentrate on my reading out there."

"That's cool, bro," Ricky responds, "let us know if you need anything."

"I sure will, homeboys. Thanks."

Right after dinner, I head outside for recreation with Isidro, Eddie, and Thomas. Smiley and Vaquero catch up with us at the running track. We warm up together for a few minutes, then everyone breaks off treading at their own pace. During my second lap, Brains joins up with me.

"What's up, brother," I greet him between heavy breaths.

"Not much," he falters. His facial expression reveals a certain distress, the kind that cannot be concealed.

"What's wrong?" I ask, "You wanna talk?"

"Yeah, but, is this a good time for you?"

"Of course, man, let's sit down over there."

We both stop to drink some water before making our way to a steel bench located behind the basketball court. Brains lowers his eyes as if he were ashamed of something. He makes a long pause, then sadly speaks, "I grew up an orphan and always lived a lonely life..."

I give him my full attention as he sheds a few tears. Brains' story is like many others. His sufferings, like mine, seem to find their origins in the remnants of a deplorable childhood. He's also a man without identity, unwanted, unloved, unable to make friends or relate to others. His eyes reflect a certain sense of worthlessness, a fear of the world.

"To be honest," he continues more calmly, "I'm not even Christian, but just seeing how the men in our group share everything with each other, makes me wanna believe in the possibility of turning the prison into a safe haven."

"Most of the guys in the group," I tell him, "have a tragedy to tell, and maybe that's the reason why we get along so well. The guys have taught me about solidarity and many other things I didn't know before. Their friendship has shown me that God is real, and if you really wanna stay with us, even if you're not Christian, you know you're more than welcome. Manu said the other day that the real message isn't about religion but love; to love everyone regardless of their religious traditions, because we were created to love and to be loved."

"I think I like that," he stutters gloomily. "Thanks,

Michael. I'm grateful to God for putting all of you in my life."

"So am I, homeboy. So am I."

We remain silent for a little while, contemplating the huge walls still reflecting pale yellow sunlight. Then we stand up as a flock of shrilling crows sweep across the empty sky.

Brains and I run a final lap before returning to the compound. He seems a little better, more accepting I would say.

Back in my cage, I open my textbooks and begin to read until past midnight. Then I fall on my knees to pray for my family and my new friends, especially for Grandpa and Manu. Before going to bed, I peer through the window to look at the sky for several minutes. I can't believe how one's life can change in just a few days. Emmanuel has opened the eyes of so many people around here. His way of life, his message of love and solidarity have spread throughout the ends of the prison. Many men have great respect for him, including some of the guards. But what happened, Lord? Where is he now? Please, bring him back safe.

CHAPTER TEN

"Mr. Moreno," I hear a grating voice very early in the morning, "get out of your cell immediately."

I toss and turn in bed several times before getting up.

"We need to search your place. Step outside."

They sift through everything, hurling things all over the cave. Then they put my hands behind my back to chain them.

"Come with us!" They bark. I obey their order without questioning, walking with my head hanging until we finally stop in front of a small cell.

It's the hole.

I begin to cry silently, glowering at them.

"Don't give us that look, Mr. Moreno. You know why you're here."

I gulp deeply.

"And you ain't going anywhere till you tell us everything."

"I don't know what you're talking about."

"Oh yes, you do."

"I swear I've got nothing to say, sir."

"Then you're staying here for the rest of your sentence."

"Oh, come on, you know you can't do that."

"Of course I can. Watch!" And he slams the door with all

his might, turns the light off, and goes away without removing the handcuffs.

I begin to whisper a prayer when all of a sudden I hear the sound of some hollow footsteps approaching the door, then echoes and voices. Someone peers through the tiny window and with a flashlight shoots a blinding beam into my face. Then they cautiously enter the cell and sit down in front of me; it's doctor Shawn and the beautiful lady, doctor Carter, from the psychiatric department.

"Sorry for the intrusion," Dr. Carter immediately sputters, putting a small medical case on the table, "but we need to talk to you, Michael." The exaggerated softness in her voice and her facial expressions seem as though she is talking to a child.

"Talk to me about what?" I respond calmly, "I'm doing a lot better now. I've found some good friends, and they're helping me understand many things I didn't know how to handle before."

The two doctors look at each other, confused. One of them pulls out a small syringe from his pocket and utters, "I'm sorry, Michael."

"What is that for?" I howl furiously.

Two guards dash into the cell when I begin to grapple with the intruders. They grab my head and arms and force me to bend over, placing my face on the table. Dr. Shawn is the one who inserts the needle into my arm, and very slowly my body loses its strength.

I wake up a few hours later, feeling as if the weight of a huge rock had fallen on me. Two officers return to take me to another facility, where, to my surprise, I find my beloved cellie. He's on his knees, close to the lower bunk, praying with such concentration that he doesn't notice when the guard opens the cell door. He seems troubled, in anguish, and his sweat is like drops of blood falling to the ground.

"Homeboy," I stammer. And he turns slowly around.

"My friend," he cries softly. A thin rim of tears appears in his eyes.

"What's wrong? Are you okay?"

"Not really. Listen, Michael. Before anything happens, I want you to know that we're enmeshed in a spiritual battle. There are some dark forces fighting against us, trying to hinder the message of love we're proclaiming."

"What do you mean?" I frown, "I don't get it."

"Satan doesn't want our brothers behind these walls to know about God's great love and forgiveness for them. We must pray so we won't fall into temptation."

My jaw drops and a strange festering fear begins to invade my entire being. Is he being serious? I stare at him suspiciously, thinking deep inside he might have gone mad. I'm not sure about all this business of evil entities. However, the icy fear penetrating my soul is quite real.

"Michael," he states, "I won't be with you for much longer. You must have faith and be ready to confront what's about to come."

I gaze at him, confused, but I'm afraid to ask why.

"Come on, homeboy," he tells me, "why you look at me like that? All I want is for you to be a free human being; free from everything that prevents you from being truly happy."

He puts his hand around my neck and I give him a tight hug.

"You know I love you, homie, but what do you mean you won't be here anymore?" I dare to ask.

"There are some things you won't understand right now, but you will soon. Just promise me you'll keep up that faith."

"I promise, homie."

We kneel to pray. Suddenly, my head begins to burn and my tongue to feel thick. I quickly slump over the filthy toilet to vomit something yellowish, streams and streams, as if I had eaten a hundred noodle soups. My cellie pats my back without ceasing to pray. I cough several times, then he wipes my mouth with his handkerchief.

"What the hell was that?" I whimper, "I haven't even eaten anything."

Without saying a word, Manu lays his hands on my head and closes his eyes.

A few minutes later, a harsh strike on the door interrupts the peace that had begun to envelop our hearts. It's the lieutenant and one of his bodyguards. They open the door and throw a brown paper bag with two apples in it, a piece of bread and a small carton of juice.

"Make it fast," Ibarra grunts, "you're going back to your place, at least for now."

Manu takes out the bread and breaks it, giving thanks to God; then he hands me a piece and takes the juice, also thanking God.

When we're through, two officers walk us back to our compound.

Our friends immediately embrace the two of us, making a fuss all over the unit. Manu and I rejoice with them as the officer in charge calls out a warning to maintain order.

"I knew you'd be back, my friend," Grandpa declares, "I never lost my faith."

"Thank you, Mr. Johnson."

Big Bear exclaims, "I wish I knew who snitched on us so I could..." and he thumps the bench.

Manu smiles but reiterates, "Thanks, brother, but remember to love your enemies and to pray for them. If you only love those who love you, why should God reward you?"

"My bad, you're right."

Now Necio and some of his men begin to argue among themselves. My cellie sits up on the bench and, assuming great authority, preaches to those who gather around him. Many other prisoners, upon hearing his voice, also crowd around to listen to him.

"Do not judge others," Manu proclaims, "so that God will not judge you, because God will judge you in the same way you judge others, and He will apply the same rules to you that you apply to others."

When he finishes declaring this and many other things, the inmates become amazed at the way he teaches. Many of them follow him to the recreation area. There, while he's still preaching, a man suffering from epilepsy approaches him, kneels down before him and says, "Sir, if you want to, you can heal me."

Everyone looks at the man, then at my cellie, and without hesitating, Emmanuel answers, "I do want to. Be healed!"

Everyone is astonished. Many of them rejoice and give thanks to God as others deem him possessed by an evil spirit. This is what they say as they leave: How can a prisoner like us, a *cholo* covered in tattoos have such powers? But many others draw near the area, bringing a crippled prisoner. My cellie touches his leg and in a matter of seconds the man recovers the strength he once had. "Your faith has made you well, my friend," Manu whispers in his ear. And once again, the crowd becomes astounded.

Then two homosexuals push their way through the multitude, crawling on their hands and knees while sobbing uncontrollably. One of them embraces Manu's feet while the other kisses his hands. My cellie helps them up, hugs them tightly, and then kisses their foreheads.

"Why are you crying?" he asks tenderly, "Of all the people gathered here, you're the ones who have loved the most. Go in peace," and he kisses them again.

Now a bunch of guards who have been watching from afar walk toward us. The officers in the towers shoot a few bullets in the air with the intention to break up the gathering, but nobody moves a foot. Then they aim at the ground, and with these shots the crowd begins to take cover. My cellie and I and the rest of our friends remain standing, close to each other.

"Who's Emmanuel?" One of the guards growls, like a fierce animal coming out of its cage.

"I am," Manu responds softly, with a blend of confidence and peace in his voice.

"Who the heck is Emmanuel?" Another officer inquires, raising his voice and aiming at us with his rifle.

"I've already told you that I am."

Two correctional officers pound him in the head, making him drop to the ground. As they try to tie him up, Big Bear and I jump on them and with all our might grab them by their necks and toss them against a bench like sacks of potatoes. The other guards immediately surround us while the shooting in the air from the men in the watchtowers continues. The first impact is a punch to my stomach which knocks the wind out of me, then a fist to my nose. Big Bear is hit right in the face with a rifle, falling at once on my side, then countless bright stars blink before my eyes. The officers kick and pummel the two of us mercilessly again and again with rifle butts until my cellie recovers enough and condemns our behavior.

"Enough!" He screams as countless troops begin to invade the area, "Haven't you two learned that those who use violence will never have the opportunity to see the other side of the world again?"

Eddie comes near Manu to help him sit on the bench while the rest of our brothers tenderly beg that we stop resisting. When we give in, our hands and feet are immediately shackled.

Then, suddenly, at the other end of the field, a few men yell with all their strength, "Man down! Man down!"

Apparently a bullet coming from the officers in the watchtowers hit a prisoner and he is being dragged to a nearby bench, his toes carving a furrow in the dust. He seems to beg for help but no words are audible. One of the guards calls for assistance through his radio as the others threaten the rest of us with the usual cursing words.

"Oh, my God," my friend Isidro mutters in the midst of the commotion, "I can't believe it. It's…"

Bursts of restless wind muffle his last words, but he looks intently at me, desiring to tell me who it is that got shot.

The squadron now has everyone on the ground, aiming their weapons here and there. Suddenly, my cellie stands up and with a great calmness defies the squad surrounding him. "Please," he tells them, "let me help that poor man."

"Help?" one of them snaps, "how are you gonna help him?"

Manu walks towards the injured prisoner.

"Stop right there!" they yell all at once. But my cellie ignores their command. "Stop!"

Then a few of them run after him, but as they get close to him, lieutenant Ibarra suddenly appears and orders them to allow him to aid the man. "Let's see what he does," he murmurs in a skeptical tone.

Everyone focuses their attention on Emmanuel who turns the riot into a mystical experience. He touches the bleeding wound of the man, which is close to his heart, and then caresses his head. He whispers something in his ear and helps him up. Then a strange silence takes over the entire place as everyone is shocked upon seeing that the recovered man is Necio, that conceited prisoner who believes himself to be the incarnation of immortality. He falls on his knees, with his jaw quivering, and tears stream down his face as he wrestles with his unbelief. This is completely incongruous; Necio, the tough guy, with a sheet of tears shining down his face. Unbelievable!

Now many prisoners who had been doubtful about Emmanuel immediately gather around him and begin to praise God, but the astonished troops, along with the lieutenant, order everyone to line up and return to our respective compounds. Necio remains with Ibarra outside while Manu is taken to an isolated cell.

Back in the unit, Smiley, Elmo, and Vaquero quickly prepare a couple of noodle soups for Big Bear and I while Roger and Ricky bring two cups of tea. We moan as we struggle to sit down. Countless bruises now cover most of our bodies.

"I'm still speechless," Grandpa explains, "There is no doubt that anything is possible for those who believe in God." Then he turns to us, "I'm sorry for what happened to you, fellows."

"It don't matter," Big Bear responds, "what matters now is that Manu gets back here safe."

"Did everyone see Necio's reaction when Manu put his hand on his wound to heal him?" Brains asks with exaggerated amazement.

"I think it was remarkable seeing that other side of him," Grandpa responds, "I've always believed that behind a tough mask there is one of tenderness."

I secretly agree with Grandpa. Something tells me Manu healed something more than just his physical wound. My cellie touched and healed the wounds that cannot be seen, the ones that putrefy the spirit.

"God is working, fellas," Eddie states, "and we must be grateful for that."

We all rejoice, joining hands while Grandpa leads us in prayer. Then officer Martinez announces something on the intercom that makes us all fall apart; they're moving everybody around into different units.

"Pack up all your belongings right away," he tells us over and over again like a programmed machine, "you don't have much time."

My friends and I turn our gaze to each other, astonished, unable to say anything. And like children who aren't allowed to play, some prisoners gather around the officer's glass box to complain, but all they get is a shrug.

"This ain't happening," Thomas finally mumbles, "What's gonna happen to our brotherhood?"

"It's not fair, man," Ricky adds.

"Oh, come on, you guys," Grandpa exclaims, then squeezes his head as a horrible twinge pricks his head, "Stop complaining. This is the perfect opportunity to go to another place and proclaim the Good News!"

Although we agree with him deep inside, we cannot help feeling a certain nostalgia. My friend Isidro grips my shoulder gently, biting his lips in fear. I get up and give him a tight hug, then the rest imitates our gesture, blessing each other goodbye.

I walk towards my cell, absorbed in a fog of uncertainty. Suddenly, the main door slides open and the appearance of lieutenant Ibarra makes me stop in my tracks. I feel chills go up and down my spine when I see that right behind him stand Necio and two other escorting officers.

"What the…" I whisper.

"Moreno," Ibarra yells, "don't make any move, you're staying here."

His news doesn't have any effect on me because my eyes have locked themselves into Necio's. He keeps staring at me like someone who has lost his memory. His eyes are clouded with tears of guilt and confusion. For a moment he appears to be an impostor. I've always believed that this man has no feelings at all.

Grandpa comes up to me. "That's good news, my boy," he stammers, "I'm also staying here."

"Really? How do you know?"

"The officer just motioned me to stay."

I smile, then wince.

"I'm going to my cell," he tells me, "I'm a little tired, and my head is killing me again. You must be really hurting, too; get some rest."

"I will, Grandpa. Have a good night. And, please, if you need anything just let me know. You have no idea how much it hurts me to see you suffer like that."

"I'll be fine, my boy. Don't worry. I'll see you tomorrow."

"God bless you, Grandpa."

I lock myself in the cave and slowly collapse on my bunk, with a million thoughts in my head. My Lord, what do you want from me? Who is this man Emmanuel? Was it you who sent him?

"I want you to be a free human being," Manu's words repeat themselves in my head, "Forgiveness. Love. Solidarity."

I shake my head as a knock on my door jolts me back to reality. I splatter some water on my face and neck before opening.

I try not to look impressed by the presence of the person in front of me, but it's impossible. There, carrying a bunch of things and with a nervous smile is one of the most frightening prisoners; Necio. He looks at me with a glimmer of goodwill in his eyes. It is a face of repentance.

"I know you might not wanna talk to me," he begins a little flustered, "You don't have to. I just wanted to give this back to you."

The stuff he's holding includes a tiny radio, personal items, clothes, and even a pair of shoes.

"What do you mean 'back to you'?" I ask, with a slight irritation creeping into my words; and he hangs his head.

"Mr. Johnson gave me all this and more to leave you alone, to stop messing with you. Look, Michael, I know I've done horrible things. And I'm really sorry for what I've done to you."

I can't avoid the look of disgust that sweeps over my face, but I try to control myself. Who am I to judge him? Haven't I done terrible things myself? Then, very slowly, tears rise in his eyes, crest his eyelids, and course down his cheeks.

"I don't want 'em," I tell him, gulping deeply. "You can keep 'em."

"It's okay," his voice strains with profound feeling, "I just hope that one day you'll be able to forgive me."

Those last words penetrate my heart like a cold dagger. What should I tell him, Lord, when you have forgiven seventy times seven my own mistakes?

"There's nothing to forgive, homeboy, but if it makes you feel better, I do forgive you."

His tears increase as a lump in his throat seems to choke him. I put my hand on his shoulder and whisper, "You may go in peace, homeboy."

"Thanks, Michael, I really needed to hear that." Then he slowly turns around and heads back to his cell with his head hanging. I sigh heavily before shutting the door.

Early in the morning, a slight squeak from the door's hinges interrupts the quietness of my sleep. A new inmate has just arrived. He quickly inspects the cave without saying anything, flings his belongings to the floor, and crawls up to the upper bunk.

I get dressed and, nostalgically, empty Manu's locker, stashing his things in my own storage.

"Hey, Mikey!" the new inmate says, almost screaming. I've never seen him before. His eyes are reddish and his corpulent anatomy, along with the vampire-looking teeth, could scare the crap out of anybody.

"How you doing?"

"Doing fine, I guess," I respond coldly.

"I hope you don't mind my staying here, in this cell."

"Why would I?" I challenge.

"Because I know everything about you and Manu."

Everything? What is he talking about? I look at him, distrustfully, and the more I stare the more maliciously he smiles. He hops down from his bed and stands in front of me with a threatening countenance. He's taller than me, a bit younger, and covered in tattoos from the neck down.

"I wanna be your friend, too," he mocks, bursting in an evil kind of laughter.

I turn around and, without uttering a word, leave him standing there, cracking his knuckles. The compound looks the same, but the entities that now wail around the tank are others. I walk towards the TV area while hundreds of wandering eyes begin to scan my movements. Some of the windows are misted over and the sun seems to be wrapped around a bunch of dense clouds. It's one of those sad suns that no one pays attention to.

"Hey, son," I hear Grandpa's quivering voice behind me, "what are you doing?"

"Nothing, just thinking."

There is something deeply wrong with him. The spark in his eyes is gone and his face is now utterly pale.

"Are you okay?" I ask, gripping his shoulder, and he coughs several times before responding.

"I have something to tell you, and it's gotta be now before it's too late."

"Come on, Grandpa, don't scare me."

"Let's go to my cell," he manages to mumble between repressed moans, "there's no one there right now."

I follow him to his place, and, as we enter, he falls to the ground as if he had been stricken by lightning. "Oh, God," I scream, bending over to help him up. "Grandpa, come on, tell me what's wrong. You want me to call the meds?"

"It's too late for that, son," he stammers, his voice muffled. "I think this is the end of everything."

"Oh, man, please, don't say that."

"Michael, I had a horrible night. I couldn't sleep at all

because I was looking for a way to tell you this without causing you any more pain."

"What are you talking about?"

The cell seems to shrink as the old fellow gasps for air. He holds my hand and asks me to sit down on the edge of the bunk. Then a dead silence takes over and overpowers even the unbridled uproar of the inmates in the common area. I lay my hand on his forehead and gently caress his face. With this gesture he begins to cry desperately, as though he didn't deserve the touch of my hands.

"I didn't wanna tell you this before," Grandpa finally expresses, gazing intently at me, "because I was hoping for a miracle..." He stops to inhale deeply but coughs. "I... I have terminal cancer, son. And... I don't wanna die without saying... how truly sorry I am for..."

My eyes begin to drown in a river of tears, and without releasing my friend's hand I kneel down before him to kiss his forehead, then his hand. His heartbreaking sobs increase and his voice loses its clarity.

"What are you sorry for, Grandpa?" I inquire softly, close to his ear.

As Grandpa begins to mumble a few words, the door is forced open by my new cellmate. He looks strangely angry, like a fierce animal ready to attack, and his red eyes seem to distill flames of hatred and scorn.

"Are you really that stupid?" he barks. "Don't you know who this bastard is?" And he points at Grandpa with his hand open. Then he hurls my friend Manu's yellow envelope at me with all his might and orders me to pull out the old fragments of newspaper hidden in the package.

"Look at them!" he shouts furiously.

I immediately examine the individuals in each of the pieces of newspaper and read the inscription below their mug shots. I feel as if a bucket of freezing water is poured over me when I notice that one of the men in the pictures is Grandpa,

Matthew Johnson. And he's been imprisoned for...

It takes me a while to assimilate the shocking news, but as soon as the truth sinks in, I painfully begin to fall apart. No! No! It can't be. I look at Grandpa, then at his mug shot. He looks younger and thinner, and although a short beard covers his face, his eyes and aquiline nose are unmistakable. It's him.

The new inmate laughs uncontrollably, and, walking towards me, he begins to hum a children's song while my entire being seems to evaporate, becoming shapeless and colorless.

"Come on, sweetheart!" the intruder grunts, "tell your boy who you really are."

I feel the blood freezing very slowly in my veins when Grandpa pulls up his shirt with his tremulous hands and shows me a tattoo of a black skull with a serpent coming out of its open jaw. It's the same tattoo of the man who sexually abused me when I was a child.

My screaming soul immediately tries to escape my body. The air becomes thick and hot, extremely hot, as though the cell were sitting on the coils of the earth, at the very mouth of hell.

"Oh, God. Please, no! No!" I yell, shuddering.

"Oh, yes," mocks the huge inmate, now leaning against the door.

Grandpa keeps staring at me, panting, with a deformed face bathed in tears; he mumbles something but the sound of his words is empty. It is his eyes that beg me to forgive him. I grip his neck with all my strength but his body begins to convulse horribly, making me back away in terror.

"Kill him!" the other prisoner shouts, "that's what you've always wanted."

"No!" I scream between soul-shredding sobs. I pull my hair violently and bump my head against the wall once, twice, and with the third blow I lose consciousness for a moment.

When I recover, Grandpa is breathing his last and the evil prisoner is sitting on the upper bunk, mockingly swinging his feet. I feel breathless, as if the air were avoiding my nostrils, and I no longer feel anything; only the voices, many of them, echoing inside my head.

"Michael," Grandpa makes a last effort, "it's okay… kill… me. I… deserve it."

I gaze at him with a mixture of disgust and compassion as tears begin to emerge once again, streams and streams of them.

"No!" I wail at the top of my voice, "No! No!"

"Kill him! Kill him! Kill him!" I hear countless voices all at the same time, and then an evil laughter permeating through the walls. I cover my ears and drag myself to the door, feeling my entire being sinking into a bottomless swamp.

"No! No! No!" I scream as loud as I can.

Suddenly, a group of men dressed in long, white smocks shove the door open and harshly grip my arms and legs, forcefully wrapping me in a straitjacket. One of them quickly prepares a syringe with a sedative substance which is then plunged into my skin. My heart immediately stops beating, and it seems as if time and the breath of life stop with it, making me meander in another world, very far from the razor wire.

A few hours later, I wake up in the same room, with my hands shackled and my head deflated, empty. Doctor Carter is sitting next to me, motionless, and several officers protect the entrance. She clears her throat before speaking, "Can you tell me your name?"

She waits patiently for my response but my words won't come out. I don't remember anything. "Do you know where you are?" she insists, calmly.

And as I anxiously gaze around, lieutenant Ibarra shows

up, and, in a matter of seconds, a huge wave of memories begins to invade my head.

"My name's Michael Moreno," I finally whisper, making an effort to withhold my tears. "Where's Grandpa? Where's Manu and my friends?"

"Sweetheart," the young lady says gently, as though she were talking to a small child, "I'm sorry, but your name is Fernando, not Michael. You're…" And she is interrupted by Doctor Shawn who enters without permission.

"You're wasting your time, Keesha," he exclaims.

I stare at both of them, utterly confused.

"Go ahead, tell him the truth again for the umpteenth time," he advises, looking at me repulsively. But my feeble mind is unable to understand such words.

"Honey," she tells me hopelessly as they all get ready to leave, "you're not just in prison; this is a mental unit. You've been in solitary confinement for seven years, and you've never had a cellmate."

ABOUT THE AUTHOR

I am just a follower of the truth.

www.ingramcontent.com/pod-product-compliance
Lightning Source LLC
Chambersburg PA
CBHW061245170626
46809CB00007B/2846